"See anything you like?" Austin drawled

Dinah turned on her heel and opened her mouth to tell him that she'd heard that line before. Why, maybe even a dozen times.

But Austin was standing much closer than she anticipated. Actually, they were standing so close that she could smell his cologne. And the starch on his shirt. And the worn leather of his old, scruffy boots. And, well, everything else about him that made him distinctly Austin Wright.

Reading her mind, he grinned slowly. "Brings back old memories, doesn't it?"

Dinah's chin snapped up. "I don't know what you're talking about."

A fresh set of lines showed up at the corners of his eyes. "Sure you do...and I do, too." Leaning so close that it was almost uncomfortable, he whispered, "Remember when we used to see each other at the honky tonks? When we used to flirt a little too much? Stand a little too close?"

Oh, she remembered a whole lot of things, all right. Maybe too many for her own good.

Dear Reader,

I don't exactly recall when my father first got Jet, his beautiful palomino. I do recall that we all thought Jet was a wonderful horse, and though I was very allergic to him, I'd sometimes walk with my dad to the barn or one of the pastures and visit him.

Jet's life with my dad was fairly sedate. My dad would ride him when he could. Otherwise Jet lived a life of semiretirement, grazing and resting. By the time I was a senior in high school, my father was fairly involved in the Houston Livestock Show and Rodeo. Because of that, he was invited to ride in the arena one evening. So off Jet went to the Astrodome! I was sitting in the stands (loaded up with Benadryl), camera in hand, and then, all of a sudden, there they were. My dad and Jet on the Astrodome's big screen! It would be hard to say who looked prouder—my dad or that horse.

I thought a lot about that moment when I wrote this book. I think there's a time in everyone's life when he or she is ready to shine, to have a second chance for glory. I did my best to let Austin and Dinah have that moment in this novel.

I can't tell you what an honor it's been to be a part of this continuity. I'm grateful for the other authors for their advice, and to our amazing team of editors for their guidance.

I hope you enjoy the book! And I'm as anxious as you to read *Beau: Cowboy Protector* by Marin Thomas, the next installment of the Harts of the Rodeo series!

Shelley Galloway

Austin:
Second Chance Cowboy

SHELLEY GALLOWAY

HARLEQUIN®
entertain, enrich, inspire™

Recycling programs
for this product may
not exist in your area.

ISBN-13: 978-0-373-75425-0

AUSTIN: SECOND CHANCE COWBOY

ABOUT THE AUTHOR

Shelley Galloway grew up in Houston, Texas, left for college in Colorado, then returned to Dallas for six years. After teaching lots and lots of sixth graders, she now lives with her husband, aging beagle and barking wiener dog in southern Ohio. She writes full-time. To date, Shelley has penned more than thirty novels for various publishers, both as Shelley Galloway for the Harlequin American Romance line, and as Shelley Shepard Gray for Avon Inspire.

Her novels have appeared on bestsellers lists. She won a Reviewers' Choice Award in 2006 and a Holt Medallion in 2009. Currently, she writes all day, texts her college son too much and tries not to think about her daughter going to college next year, too. Please visit her online at www.Harlequin.com or her website, www.shelleygalloway.com.

Books by Shelley Galloway
HARLEQUIN AMERICAN ROMANCE

*Men of Red River

This book is dedicated to my fellow Harlequin Continuity Authors, Cathy, C.J., Roz, Marin, Linda. What a privilege it's been!

Chapter One

The light streaming through the cheap metal miniblinds was blinding. Austin Wright discovered if he squinted his eyes and turned his head a little to the left, he could almost stand it. Now, if he could only find a way to deal with the sickly, sweet sensation of needing to vomit.

Why the hell hadn't he stopped after those first three shots of Cuervo Gold?

Because you're a drunk, a stinging, no-holds-barred voice whispered into his ear. *Whispered* being the key phrase. Anything louder was going to cause him to run—not walk—to the bathroom and divest himself of the remaining contents of his stomach.

He almost remembered the events of last night, but wasn't quite sure. Most of those memories were forever lost in a blackout. Austin gingerly propped himself up on his elbows and began looking for evidence. He'd done this before.

Too many mornings, the voice declared, making him wince. Only the threat of spending the rest of his morning washing soiled sheets kept him from lying back down and praying for oblivion. He'd done that before, too.

Warily, he glanced to his left. His Wranglers lay in a wad on the floor. Both his ropers were there, too.

He was just about to test turning his head to the right when a Gary Allan song started blaring from his cell phone.

Shit.

Scooting to the edge of the bed, he carefully bent down and reached a shaky hand toward his jeans. In one carnival-contortionist move, he was able to inch the denim closer, pull his cell out of the back pocket and finally punch the phone. Blessed silence.

"Yeah?" he rasped.

"Austin?" The girl's voice was as sweet as it was sinful. "Honey, you okay?"

"I'm okay," he muttered, doing his best to recall the lady's name on the other side of the phone. Sandra? Cindy?

Finally, the name clicked. Stacy.

"I'm okay, Stacy," he said, emphasizing her name. As though it was a real special thing for him to remember.

"Oh, good," she replied with a breathless sigh. "I was a little worried last night. After, you know…"

No, as a matter of fact, he had no idea what the "you know" referred to. Biting his lip, he turned to the other side of the bed, looking for any sign that a woman had slept there.

Luckily, all he saw was a Hanes T-shirt long faded to a dingy gray and a wrinkled button-down. Not a pair of panties or a lacy bra in sight.

By turns disgusted with his behavior and bolstered by the evidence that he hadn't completely gone crazy, Austin cleared his throat and went about lying with the best of them. "Stacy, I'm fine. Real fine." Suddenly worried, he added, "And you?"

A light laugh fluttered through the phone. In another time, it would have stirred up his blood pressure. "Oh, I'm fine, Austin. I enjoyed every moment of your company," she purred.

He almost relaxed. Maybe he hadn't been that big of a jackass?

"That is, I was just super—until you cashed it in all over my Ariats."

Cashed it in? It took a half second, but he finally figured out what she was referring to. Ah. He'd vomited on her boots.

Way to connect the dots, Austin.

Damn. Sitting up straighter, he ignored his pounding head, his sour stomach, the dry feeling around his tongue. Ariats were nice boots. Easily over a hundred a pop. "Listen, Stacy, about your boots. I'll pay—"

"They were just my old ropers. You and I know I've had worse than that on 'em," she said with a laugh. "Nothing to worry about."

He exhaled in relief. Because, well, he didn't have a spare dime to pay for a new pair of boots.

Because you had to go buy the whole bar a round of tequila, the voice said nastily.

"Austin, I didn't call to give you grief about my boots. I just wanted to check on you."

"Check on me?"

"Well, yeah. I was worried. I just wanted to make sure that you were, you know…okay?"

Alive, she meant. His shame was reaching new levels. She'd called to make sure he'd made it through the rest of the night. "Don't worry about me, sugar. I'm always fine."

"You sure?" she said a little hesitantly. "Because by the time we got you cleaned up and the clock struck three…you were sounding a little blue…" Her phone clicked. "Oops. I gotta go. That's Daddy. Church today, you know."

She hung up before he could respond to his blue mood or Sunday services. After clicking off his cell, too, he gripped it hard in his hand. For a moment, he was tempted to toss it across the room, but all that would do was ruin a perfectly good phone.

And he'd already ruined plenty over the past year.

His cotton mouth got drier as memories flashed. The times

he'd driven home drunk, the times he'd woken up beside women he didn't remember meeting.

The time he'd lived on ramen noodles for two weeks because he'd had to borrow money for gas in his truck. Because he'd spent every last dime at a rowdy bar in Sheridan.

With a groan, he pulled off his sheets and made himself put both feet on the floor. It was time to greet his new day.

Padding to the bathroom, he looked in the mirror. Caught himself in all his naked glory. He paid no notice to the lean muscles of his arms or the light line of hair that ran from the middle of his pecs to his belly.

He ignored the scars on his side and hands and forearms from too many falls and a whole lot of idiocy.

Instead he concentrated on the greenish-gray pallor of his face. His dry, chapped lips.

Then he looked beyond the bloodshot eyes to what he saw in them—the complete look of hopelessness.

He'd hit rock bottom, at least as far down as he was willing to go. He knew all about living with a drunk and a disappointment. He had become his own worst nightmare, and he didn't know how he was ever going to recover.

Wrapping a towel around his waist, he padded back into his bedroom, grabbed his jeans and pulled out his wallet from the back pocket.

And there, sure enough, was a business card of a tire distributor. But that wasn't what was important. Flipping it over, Austin stared at the name and phone number scrawled in a black felt-tip marker. The guy, who'd only said his name was Jack, had been in Austin's store shopping for gear, said he'd known Buddy, Austin's dad.

Further conversation revealed that Jack was a family man. He'd shown off a photo of him, his wife and two young boys posed in front of a Christmas tree. Austin had been wondering what the heck Jack had in common with him until Jack relayed that he'd almost lost it all—his business, his wife… even his kids.

When he'd handed the number to Austin and told him about the weekly meetings held right in Roundup's Congregational Church, Austin had been stunned. Never would he have guessed that this guy had ever had a drinking problem. Actually, the guy had looked as though he had more together than most folks.

Austin had copped an attitude when Jack had started talking about how the hour-long meetings had changed him. About how he'd meant every single word of that Serenity Prayer.

But long after Jack left, when no one was looking, Austin had put the card in his wallet. Just in case he was ever so weak to dial the number.

You mean brave, idiot, his conscience whispered.

"Yeah, I mean brave," he said. He sat on the edge of his mattress, picked up the phone and made himself dial before he lost his nerve. Before he turned cowardly all over again.

Finally, it was time. Finally, he was ready to do what he'd been pussyfooting around for the past three years. He was going to get some help.

"Hello!"

"Hey, Jack—"

"I'm not available right now, but leave a message. I'll call you back—I always do."

Austin didn't want to leave a message. But he wanted help more. Thinking of his father, and the way no one gave him a moment's time, he forced himself to talk.

"Jack, it's, uh… It's Austin Wright. You gave me your number a couple of months ago when you stopped by my store. In case, you know, I ever wanted to talk to you. I guess I do. Call me back." He left his cell-phone number and clicked off.

Then practically ran into the shower, needing to clean off

last night's trouble. And the doubts that were surfacing all over again.

Bracing himself for the pain, he stepped under the showerhead and turned on the water, taking the cold blast of H_2O against his skin as rightful penance.

It was no less than he deserved.

"Hey, Dinah," Duke called out. "What's shaking?"

She laughed. It had taken a while, but she and her deputy, Duke Adams, finally had the sheriff's office running smoothly. Actually, Duke was more than her deputy; he was also her cousin.

And her friend.

Truth was, Sheriff Dinah Hart needed Duke's good humor to help her get through the days in Roundup. In their small town, they got all sorts of calls. Anything could happen—from letting people into their locked cars, to directing traffic on Sundays at noon when the folks got out of church, to their current project: figuring out who in the world was involved with the recent outbreak of thefts in the area.

"Not too much is shaking right now," she said wearily. "I'm exhausted."

"What kept you up this time?"

"Too much fun at the Open Range on the weekend." She shared a look with Duke. And though there had been more than one man letting off too much steam at Roundup's biggest bar, she let herself fixate on the one man she could never ignore. "I tell you what, sometimes I'm this close to wringing Austin Wright's neck."

Leaning against an old metal file cabinet, he crossed his arms over his chest. "What's he done this time?"

"Nothing illegal, just made a mess of the place. Again." Remembering her first call of the day, she shook her head. "Ted was fit to be tied when he called me bright and early this morning. Seems Austin puked his life out in the middle of the place on Saturday night."

Duke cocked an eyebrow. As usual, his low-key way complemented her inclination toward drama. "Don't see why he called you. Puking's unpleasant, but last I heard, it wasn't a crime."

"It wasn't just that. Two good old boys got in a fight about where a dart landed or some such nonsense. They broke a pair of chairs and seemed intent on getting their hands on those darts for darker reasons."

Duke winced.

"Yeah. It got ugly." She sighed. "But I think Ted would've dealt with it all on his own if I hadn't just paid him a visit. Somehow I must have conveyed that truly no problem was too small for our department."

"That sounds like something you'd do."

"Actually, I think Ted just wanted someone to listen to him."

Duke curved his lips up slightly. "And you did."

Boy, had she. Shaking her head, she said, "Sorry, Duke. What you got?"

He slid a paper over her way. "Another missing bridle and saddle, this one a Silver Royal from the Neiman ranch." Whistling low, he added, "Craig Neiman says it's worth a grand. At least."

Dinah knew the prices of some saddles. And though Silver Royal was a good brand, all saddles weren't created the same.

A theft was always treated seriously, but she knew Craig Neiman had a propensity to exaggerate when he could.

She had an idea. "Look, how about I go visit with Austin and see if that estimate is correct? It's a perfect excuse to pay him a call and give him a gentle reminder about behaving himself out in public."

"While you do that, I'll go visit with the Neimans. See how the rest of their tack looks."

"Great. Call me if you need me to stop by, too."

Duke nodded. "Sounds good." Pausing on his way out, he looked back at her, his brown eyes full of brotherly concern. "You okay with seeing Austin? You've got some history there."

"That history is as old as the dartboard at the Open Range. And as full of holes, too."

Duke grinned at her reference, then sobered. "Just be careful you don't get stuck with anything, D. Those darts can hurt like a son of a gun."

So did a lot of things, she thought to herself as she grabbed her purse, her gun and a candy bar for good measure.

Experience had taught her that a bite from a Snickers bar could do a girl a world of good.

Even when seeing Austin Wright.

Chapter Two

No man should look as good as Austin Wright, Dinah decided.

Blessed with a dreamy pair of blue eyes, dark wavy hair and a striking resemblance to Blake Shelton, he'd stopped more than one girl in her tracks. A long time ago, she'd kissed him in the moonlight on the outskirts of town.

That kiss had been hot enough to make her step back in a hurry. And hot enough to make Austin smile just a little too darkly.

Though she'd surely kissed other men since—and Austin had done a whole lot more with a whole lot more girls—that kiss never failed to pop up in her memory whenever they crossed paths.

It was a real shame, too.

"Hey, Dinah," he said as she stepped into his shop, Wright's Western Wear and Tack. "You're a sight for sore eyes. You need something?"

Oh, that drawl! She blinked, and before she knew it, she was smoothing her left hand down the front of her tan sheriff's shirt.

"No. I'm not here to shop."

"Oh?" Gone went that teasing glint in his eyes. "What do you need?"

His voice was low. Gravelly and cool. And it affected her like it always had—with a zing right to her middle.

With effort, she opened up her spiral notebook and pretended to study her notes so he wouldn't see her expression.

And so she wouldn't start thinking about his blue eyes. And the way he did love to wear those Wranglers of his just a little low and a little tight. "I did come in here for something."

"What?"

Lifting her chin, she strived for confidence and equilibrium. "I came to see what you knew about Silver Royal saddles."

"For riding or show?"

"Show."

"Other than they cost the earth?"

"Are they that much? I mean, how much earth are we talking about?"

"Easily a grand." He looked at her curiously. "Why? You gonna start showing horses or something?"

Sidestepping the questions, she edged farther into the store, her boots clicking softly on the wooden floor. Took a peek toward the back of the shop where the tack was organized. "Any chance you got one of them around? My family never believed in spending that much on a saddle." Their money had always been marked for stock.

Austin shook his head. "I can't help you there, Dinah. You're looking at a one-man show here. I ain't got a lot of cause to be showcasing expensive saddles. Most folks who come in are looking for something a little more practical— more like something from King."

Looking around a little more closely, Dinah realized she'd never spent much time in the place. Not enough to really study his merchandise, anyway.

In the front of the store there was a decent selection of shirts and Carhartt coats. A couple of racks of socks and gloves and hats. In the back was the "tack" section. Hanging neatly on pegs were bridles and reins, bits and cinches. Some new, but mostly used.

There were also six saddles. Even from the front, she could tell they'd seen a lot of action. Kind of like the man in front of her, she thought wryly.

She walked on back. Austin followed. "You here on official business?" he asked. "Or do you suddenly have a yen for a fancy new saddle?"

She thought everyone and their brother knew her family was having financial difficulties—like the rest of Montana. Plus, with her job and all, she never had time to ride.

Correction, she'd never taken the time to ride. "Business."

"I see."

Did he?

Her brothers expected her to be tough. The folks who'd elected her counted on her to be that way. The city council certainly paid her to be. But Austin? He was looking as though it would make his day if she revealed she was just a woman. Just like the girl she'd used to be, before she got her act together and figured out what she really wanted in life— to be respected.

Her mouth went dry as she looked blankly at the merchandise surrounding them. When was the last time she'd even thought about being just a girl? Just Dinah?

"See anything you like?" he drawled from behind her back.

She turned on her heel, opened her mouth to give him what for, to tell him that she'd heard that line before. Why, maybe even a dozen times.

But he was standing a whole lot closer than she anticipated. Actually, they were standing so smack-dab close that she could smell his cologne. And the starch on his shirt. And the worn leather of his old, scruffy boots and belt. And, well, everything else about him that made him distinctly Austin Wright.

Reading her mind, he grinned slowly. "Brings back old memories, don't it?"

Her chin snapped up. "I don't know what you're talking about."

A fresh set of lines showed up at the corners of his eyes. "Sure you do…and I do, too." Leaning so close that it was almost uncomfortable, he whispered, "Remember when we used to see each other at the honky-tonks? When we used to flirt a little too much? Stand a little too close?"

Oh, yes, she did. At any age, Austin Wright had held the right combination of heat and bad-boy charm that she'd always found next to irresistible.

Back when she'd been eighteen? She hadn't even tried to deny a thing with him.

Lifting a hand, he curved a stray lock of hair around her ear. "D, remember when we danced to Bon Jovi and thought we were cool?"

Glad for the memory, she laughed. "I was an idiot. I used to wear ridiculous band T-shirts."

His grin widened as he stepped back and gave them a bit more breathing room. "And tight jeans. No one could fill out those Levi's like you could."

Yes, she had worn them tight. But then, so had he. And he still did.

Still reminiscing, he murmured, "You had a lot of hair back then."

It had fallen to the middle of her shoulder blades. She'd kept it curly and a little wild. Now she kept her dark hair tamer. Every morning, she ruthlessly transformed the out-of-control curls to gentle waves that rested on the tops of her shoulders.

Before she knew it, she was fingering the end of a wayward curl. She had loved her long hair. But it was best she didn't look like that anymore. No one would have taken a woman like that seriously.

"You had quite a head of hair, too," she countered.

He ran a hand along his neck. "I like mine short now." He cracked a smile. "But we thought we were all that and a bag of chips back in those days. Remember?"

She did. Oh, she remembered a whole lot of things. The way they used to hang out together when they'd be off at some of the local rodeos. No matter how much she'd promised her mother she'd behave, before long, she and Austin would egg each other on. Next thing she knew, she was dodging her brothers' watchful eyes and sneaking around to where the trailers were parked. There, they'd sit in the dark, smoke a little, drink a whole lot more. One time they finally had given in to their attraction and shared that one amazing kiss.

Damn! That was the second time she'd thought of that in two hours!

With effort, she pushed aside all those feelings of desire… and remembered also how she'd finally decided it was time to grow up and become respectable. And Austin?

He hadn't made that choice yet. Maybe he wouldn't ever want to stop his partying and his women and his idiocy. Which meant they had nothing in common now.

Which kind of made her sad, and that was more than a little distressing!

Turning away, she patted one of the saddles. "This is beautiful."

"You've got an eye, and that's a fact. Just got that one in."

"Who from?"

He looked evasive. "A woman out near Miles City."

Tenderly, she ran her finger along the initials etched in the leather. "Any special reason why she sold it?"

"Nah. Her family fell on hard times. Had to sell the horse…" He shrugged. "The saddle came next."

She bit her lip. Bringing back memories of barrel racing, feeling the wind against her hair. Feeling sweat running down her back as she tried to beat the clock.

And how she'd given up riding but hadn't ever asked her family to sell that saddle.

That shamed her. Who knows? The money might have come in real handy lately. Her brother Ace could've probably used the money to pay for some of Midnight's feed. Or the ranch's electric bill. But she'd been too intent on keeping her saddle to think about that. No, she'd been selfishly holding on to it, as if she couldn't bear to completely forget all of her past.

"Want to go riding one day, Dinah?"

"No."

"Sure? We could go to my dad's." His voice was bright now. Less suggestive, almost friendly. Almost cheerful. "I haven't been out to see him lately, but I do know Dad's still keeping a couple of horses. Some of 'em are top-notch. Riding for a few hours, forgetting our troubles? It would be fun."

Mention of his dad made her think of the other little reason she'd come visiting.

"So, I heard you created quite a mess at the Open Range."

His voice turned flat. "Bad news travels fast."

"Always."

He tilted his head to one side. "Is puking my brains out against the law these days?"

"No. But driving under the influence is," she said quickly. Thinking of a reason for bringing it up.

"Your mole should've told you that I didn't drive."

Oops. She hadn't even asked. "Who did?"

He shook a finger at her as though she was a naughty child. "Uh-uh, Dinah. No way am I going to tell you all my secrets. That ain't no business of yours."

"Look, Ted doesn't care to be cleaning up those messes of yours."

"I realize that." His blue eyes narrowed. "And I hope when you spoke to old Ted that he also told you that I stopped by this morning and offered to pay for the cleaning."

"He didn't tell me that." Irritation surged through her. If Ted had taken the time to whine to her, why the heck hadn't he felt like telling her the whole story? "But you were drinking shots of tequila, weren't you?"

"I do believe I was. Sheriff."

Now she felt worse than a prude. Her job was to uphold the law, not become the moral majority. "I just wanted to make sure, you know, that you weren't going to make overdoing it…a habit."

"No, ma'am."

A lot of men called women "ma'am," but rarely in that tone of voice.

She backed up a step. His eyes were cool and hard now. Reminding her that she'd just crossed the line and hadn't really played fair, either. Using friendship to get information wasn't anything she was proud of.

Just as she was turning around, she glanced at the saddles again.

And happened to see a lightly tanned one, with roses hand tooled along the skirt.

She knew that saddle. And last time she heard, the owner had reported it missing.

She headed to the door before he noticed her staring at it. She needed to get more information before she asked him about its origins. One of the first things she'd learned at the police academy was to try not to ask questions you didn't already know the answers to. "Look, thanks for the information about the Silver Royals. I'll be seeing you, Austin," she called out over her shoulder.

"Feel free to stop by anytime and give me grief."

His words hit a nerve. She hoped he didn't notice her stumble. Pushing open the glass door, she strode out and into her cruiser.

And as she drove down the main street through town, she grimaced with sad satisfaction. Suddenly, everything was starting to make sense. Austin Wright was a small-business owner and no doubt was struggling to keep a solid inventory. He was probably having money trouble—most everyone in the county was. Then, of course, there was the Wright name. It had practically become synonymous with sketchy practices. Why, everyone knew his daddy had spent time in jail.

Had Austin decided to start making money the easy way? If he had, and if he was now bound and determined to start following in his father's footsteps…well, there was probably little he wouldn't do.

She hated to think that way about him. But they weren't really friends anymore. And she was far different from the girl she used to be when they were.

She needed to remember that.

Chapter Three

"I'm so glad you had time to meet with me, Flynn," Dinah said as they took a seat in one of the booths at the Number 1 Diner. Though it hadn't been in Roundup for all that long, every time Dinah entered the place she felt a burst of nostalgia. It probably had something to do with the old photos of miners decorating the walls.

Or maybe it was the bright cherry-red Formica tabletops. Or maybe seeing waitresses dressed in jeans and boots and those red-and-black aprons just made her smile. "I had a real need for girl time."

"I'm always up for a cheeseburger, you know that. Carbs and saturated fat can do a world of good for a woman in the throes of pregnancy."

Looking at her friend and sister-in-law with a real fondness, Dinah laughed. "One thing never changes, Flynn. Come hell or high water, you're never afraid to tell it like it is. Even if it involves too much information."

"It's only TMI if people don't care," she said, rubbing her growing belly. "And I'm sure you do care."

"I'm taking the Fifth on that one." Grinning, she opened the plastic menu and skimmed over the choices, lingering on the idea of a burger and fries…then resolutely focusing on the salads and grilled chicken. She'd worked too hard at the police academy to ignore the physical regime and exams.

No way was she going to slide down into a slippery slope of unhealthy choices.

By the time Karla stopped at their table, chomping her ever-present gum, Dinah had made her decision. "I'll have the Cobb salad, dressing on the side, Karla."

"Drink?"

"Diet."

Flynn made gagging noises. "That's what I love about you, Dinah. You're nothing if not predictable. Karla, I'll have a cheeseburger, fries and a chocolate shake."

Karla winked. "Gotcha. Sure you don't want to change your mind and get something with a couple of more calories, Dinah?"

What she wanted and could have were two different things. And, well, there was that secret stash of Snickers bars she couldn't seem to ignore. "I'm good. Thanks." Looking around, Dinah tried to catch sight of Sierra Byrne, the owner of the diner. "Karla, where's Sierra?"

Karla shifted uneasily. "I'm not sure. Maybe she's with her aunt Jordan? Sometimes Sierra and Jordan take Molly out on walks together."

Dinah vaguely recalled seeing Sierra's aunt Jordan and her Seeing Eye dog, Molly, walking in the park. "Oh. Well, tell Sierra 'hey' next time you see her."

"Will do."

When they were alone, Flynn crossed her arms over her chest. "So, you want to tell me why you called?"

"I just wanted lunch. And I wanted to hear how things were going at the ranch. And with the veterinary practice, too."

"I'm sure Ace's been keeping you informed." Raising a brow, she said, "Ace said he talked to you about everything a few days ago. Did he actually call you?"

All her brothers called her on a regular basis—well, all except Tuf, she realized with a sinking heart. Ever since he was discharged from the marines, all they knew about Tuf was that he was somewhere in America. And that he had no desire to come to Roundup, Montana.

However, when Colt or Ace did call to check in, it was a bare-bones thing. They checked up on her. They filled her in with ranch news, all the time giving her a subtle reminder that she should be stopping by the house a whole lot more than she did.

"Ace called," Dinah said. "Ace always calls."

Flynn tilted her head to the side. As she did so, her blond hair shimmered a bit. Reminding Dinah of how healthy and vibrant she looked in her pregnancy. "So you just decided to ask me to lunch? Out of the blue?"

Why was Flynn making such a big deal about this? "A girl's got to eat."

"That is true. But you? On a Monday? I don't think so."

What the heck?

"Flynn, you're making it seem like I don't eat." Looking down at her jeans, she privately wished they were a little less loose. She'd been losing weight something awful with the way the case was going. Or not going. "I do."

"That is true. But you always stay in your office and file during lunch on Mondays."

With some surprise, Dinah realized her sister-in-law was exactly right. She'd regimented her life so well that even people she didn't see very often knew her schedule. All in an attempt to always be in control.

Pushing that thought away, she decided to dive into the deep end and hope Flynn had enough strength of character to pull her out while she was still breathing. "I saw Austin Wright today," she blurted.

"Austin, huh?" Flynn picked up the shake that had just been delivered and took a healthy sip. "And this means something because…"

"You know how we used to be friends." When Flynn just kept staring, Dinah finished the thought. "Okay. Really good friends."

"We live in a small town. Everybody here has been friends with each other at one time."

Flynn had a point, but it also wasn't exactly true. A lot of them had been friends. And a lot of them had hung around together. But not so much with Austin or his sister, Cheyenne. In fact, apart from a span of eight months when she'd decided to live on the wild side, she'd never had much to say to him.

Well, she'd never trusted herself to have much to say to him.

Her mother had never been a real big fan of her seeing Austin, and with good reason, too.

"You know how everyone is around Austin," Dinah added, not so obliquely referring to Austin's troubles with bottles of bourbon.

With a grin, Flynn fanned herself with her paper napkin. "I know he's just about the finest thing I've ever seen. Except for Ace, of course. It's hardly fair. No man should look so good."

Flynn was so right. Austin had looked good. Even all worn-out and tired-looking, he'd looked really good.

But even noticing felt like a betrayal of what she believed in. What she stood for. She needed to think about her job and her reputation. Not the wicked urges she had whenever she was around him. "I went to his shop to ask him about some saddles and we started talking," Dinah said. "Do you ever have much occasion to visit with him?"

"You mean besides when I go shopping at his store?"

To her embarrassment, Dinah had never imagined anyone actually shopping there. It had always seemed a poor substitute for someplace better.

But maybe that had been a mean excuse. Maybe she'd really just been avoiding Austin. The idea made her uncomfortable. "You've shopped in Wright's Western Wear?"

"Uh, yeah," Flynn said with a touch of sarcasm. "They sell clothes and Western wear. I like wearing clothes and Western wear. When I'm not about to have a baby."

Dinah was saved from replying to that by the arrival of her salad and Flynn's juicy cheeseburger.

As she carefully dipped a forkful of iceberg lettuce into a dab of ranch dressing, she covertly watched Flynn take a healthy bite out of that burger. As she chewed, swallowed and then chomped on a fry, Flynn's expression turned to pure bliss. No doubt it was the exact opposite of her own.

After swallowing, Flynn continued. "To answer your question, I've talked to Austin a few times at his store. But a whole lot more at rodeos." She paused, then added, "I talked to him the other day at church, too. Actually, last Sunday, we had a real nice chat."

Church? Dinah didn't know if she was more upset to discover her brother and Flynn and Austin were attending church together or that they all knew she hadn't stepped foot in a church since Christmas. "What was he like there?"

"Friendly."

"Was he acting all right?"

"We were sitting in a couple of pews during a Sunday service, Dinah. What do you think?" She scowled slightly, then took another bite of that burger. And dipped two thick French fries into a puddle of mustard and ketchup.

A little stung—probably because Flynn had a good reason for sounding so sarcastic—Dinah said, "You don't need to get snippy with me. I'm just asking questions."

"I'm getting the feeling that you're looking for trouble where there isn't any. I just told you I talked to him at church and you act like I said we met at some…some porn store."

She was glad her fork was sitting on her plate. "Porn store?"

"Oh, you know what I mean. You're looking for trouble, and frankly, it's disturbing. Just because a man's family might not be completely upstanding, it doesn't mean he doesn't have redeeming qualities."

"I know that," she said quickly.

"Do you? Maybe you've gotten too used to only looking for the worst in people, now that you're the sheriff and all."

That hurt. And, with Austin, she feared it might be true. "Let's talk about something else."

Flynn popped two more fries in her mouth. "All right."

"Tell me about everything at work. Have any puppies been brought into the clinic lately?" Even though Flynn and Ace specialized in equines, every so often someone would come in with a litter of puppies.

Flynn's eyes narrowed, but after yet another sip of her chocolate shake, she smiled. "As a matter of fact, a family brought in a litter of eight beagle pups last week." She chuckled. "Oh, Dinah, you should've seen Ace! He's so used to working with horses and cows, he hardly knew what to do when those brown, black and white fur balls got loose."

Dinah smiled at the idea of her confident, capable brother chasing wayward pups. "I bet they were cute."

"Cute as all get-out!" Patting her swollen stomach, she said, "If we weren't fixin' to have our own bundle of joy, I swear I'd have been badgering Ace to let us keep one."

Imagining a puppy of her own, something soft and sweet to cuddle, she asked, "Whose puppies were they?"

"The Morans. Do you know them?"

"I know of them, but we haven't had much of an occasion to talk."

"Are you thinking about getting a puppy? Because if you are, you should stop by Angie and Duke's place, too. I hear someone left Angie a basket of mongrel pups that are adorable. The price is right, too. They're free."

Getting a puppy was a pretty bad idea. And if she got one, it should be something dignified and policeworthy, like a German shepherd or something. After all, Duke had Zorro, and he was a great dog. But beagles were sweethearts…and abandoned mixed-breeds? They needed someone to love them. She could do that. "Maybe."

"I'll text you Kim Moran's phone number if you want. You could give her a call. Or get Duke to take you to his house and look at the free puppies. I'm sure Angie would love to visit with you a bit."

Ouch. There was another not-too-subtle reminder that she wasn't doing a very good job of keeping in touch with the family.

Smiling sweetly, Flynn said, "You know what, Dinah? I think a sweet little puppy might just be the thing for you."

"Because?"

"Because everyone needs someone to love." Looking like the loved woman she was, Flynn's eyes sparkled. "Even you, Dinah. Even a tough-as-nails sheriff like you."

Even her. Thinking about that, her heart sank. Somehow, along the way to being respectable and upstanding and respected…she'd lost a little bit of her softness.

Suddenly, she ached to get it back.

Chapter Four

"Hey, Duke?"

Her deputy spun toward her on the stool he'd just discovered in the back storage closet of their hole-in-the-wall office. "Yep?"

"Tell me the truth. Do you think Austin Wright is responsible for the string of burglaries?"

As was his nature, Duke pondered that one for a moment. "I don't want him to be. But what we want and what actually is don't do either of us a lot of good, does it?"

After crossing the room—which meant she took five steps to the left and scooted around a line of metal filing cabinets—she slumped down in her chair. "No, it doesn't." Drumming the tips of her fingers on her desk, she looked at him sideways. "How do you want to handle things?"

"I already took a picture of the saddle you saw at Wright's and sent it to Kevin Johnson. It's his wife's. And it had been stolen."

She was afraid of that. Before she thought the better of it, she blurted what was first and foremost on her mind. "For the life of me, I just can't imagine Austin stealing that saddle and then sticking it in his store."

Duke chuckled. "That does sound pretty gutsy, even for Austin."

It sounded stupid, too. And though Austin might have a

lot of problems, stupidity had never been one of them. But she felt honor bound to play devil's advocate. "I guess there's always a chance he could be working with the thieves…"

After giving Zorro a brief scratch behind his ears, Duke turned to Dinah. "Want to know what I think?"

"Of course."

"I think Austin bought it off a guy like he said he did. The people selling the merchandise are smart, Dinah. They're not stealing and selling it to the public directly."

"I hear you." But like a dog with a bone, she couldn't seem to move from her train of thought. "However, Austin could be more involved than he's letting on. It's a possibility."

"But doubtful." He paused. "You don't think he had anything to do with Midnight being stolen, do you?"

She shook her head in a kind of knee-jerk reaction of sorts. "Austin wouldn't do that. He wouldn't steal our family's prize stallion." Her brother Ace had bid on Midnight at a horse auction a few months back, and nothing around Thunder Ranch had been the same ever since. Midnight had proven to be ornery and proud and wonderful.

Her brother Colt had shown them all that Midnight had a lot more rodeos left in him, too. And then the thieves had struck their ranch, stolen her dad's beautiful saddle, some of Colt's bridles…and Midnight had gone missing.

Duke relaxed. "Boy, I'm glad to hear you say you don't suspect Austin of horse thieving. I can't see him doing it, either, but I wanted to hear the words from your lips."

She rolled her shoulders uncomfortably. Her feelings about Austin were knee-deep and confusing as all get-out. But there were some things she couldn't bear to even imagine him doing.

Stealing Midnight was one of them.

"I'll follow up on some of the leads we talked about before accusing Austin of anything."

"That sounds like a good plan to me."

Realizing that Duke didn't sound all that interested in the conversation, she looked up from her notes. "Duke, you look pleased about something. I know it's not saddles. What's up?"

"Angie and me are going away this weekend."

"What?"

To her amusement, her cousin's cheeks flushed. "Remember, we discussed calendars a couple of weeks ago? Luke is going to stay the weekend with the family at the ranch. Beau wants to spend some time with him. While they're bonding and such, I'm going to take Angie down to Casper, Wyoming."

"What a great idea." Both Duke's trip with Angie and Beau spending time with Luke sounded nice. Since Beau and Duke were twins, Dinah was glad that the wilder of the two brothers was taking so much time to get to know his nephew.

"Oh, it's not much, but it will be nice to get away. They've got a fall festival that's real popular."

"I'm sure anything you do will be fun." Dinah knew Duke loved Angie's little boy as completely as if he'd been his own son. But that didn't mean he never craved a little alone time with his new wife. "Have a good time."

"Oh, we will. And, Dinah?"

"Yeah?"

"I mean this in the best possible way... Don't call me."

She chuckled. "Don't worry, Deputy. This sheriff should be able to handle things just fine for a few days on her own. Let's just sit tight on this case for a couple of days."

"Roger that. Besides, I don't want you to deal with Austin on your own if we figure he is the man behind all our headaches."

"That sounds good. There are plenty of other things going on." Looking at the list of messages on her desk, Dinah knew that was practically an understatement.

There had been a rash of problems with some of the high school kids in the area. Nothing too serious—just some graffiti painted on the back of the bleachers of the football stadium, and a couple reports of underage parties in outlying areas.

Feeling vaguely like the pot calling the kettle black, she realized that the reports listed a lot of the same stuff she'd done during her junior year in high school. Only she might have been worse.

With a wince, she hoped Principal Marks didn't bring it up during their scheduled meeting. Carol Marks had been a new teacher when Dinah graduated high school.

Dinah remembered her being slightly shocked at Dinah's way of dressing and her behavior. Hopefully, though, Mrs. Marks would remember just how hard Dinah had worked her senior year to turn things around.

SHE WAS STUCK IN THE GROCERY store line behind a woman with way too many coupons when she spied Austin in the next checkout lane. As she was attempting to figure out how to say hi to him without making a big deal of it, he looked up and caught her eye.

While the lady's grocery bill continued to slide, fifty cents at a time, she smiled his way.

He came over, a paper sack in his left arm. "Hey," he said. "What's shaking?"

She laughed that he'd used the same expression as Duke. "Just waiting my turn. What about you? This is the last place I'd expect to see you on a Saturday night."

"I eat, too." He tapped his bag. "I've got a chicken and some potatoes just calling my name." Eyeing her groceries, displayed for all to see on the conveyor belt, he laughed. "If you eat any more of those diet dinners, you're going to float away, Dinah."

She felt her face heat. "Unlike you, I'm not much of a cook. And eating at the Number 1 all the time can get expensive."

Finally the woman in front of her paid her bill and it was Dinah's turn to check out. As the clerk started scanning and bagging, she turned to Austin again. "Hope you have a good evening."

"You, too." He turned, took two steps, then came back over to her side. "Want to come over?"

"For dinner?"

"Don't act like I'm wining and dining you, D. It's just chicken and potatoes."

His idea sounded a whole lot better than a diet frozen dinner. And there was something brewing between them that was hard to deny. "I've got a salad in a bag. I could bring that." Gosh, did she sound as lame as she felt?

"We'll have three food groups covered right there. After you take your groceries home, come over."

"All right. I will."

After presenting her with a pleased-looking smile, he turned and walked away. Dinah's eyes followed him, noticing that his jeans today were still awfully snug...and were faded and worn in all the right places.

"Thirty-eight twenty-five," the cashier said.

As Dinah handed her two twenties, the cashier winked. "I thought I was going to have to bop you on the head, Sheriff."

"And why's that?"

"Austin Wright is just about the finest-looking man in these parts. Only a fool would turn down the chance for him to make her dinner."

There was a flurry of replies on the tip of her tongue. But only one right answer. "I was kind of thinking the same thing," she admitted.

And with that, she grabbed her bags and hurried out to her car, anxious to spend some time with Austin, just to see if her instincts had been right.

Chapter Five

Sitting across from her, Austin had to admit that spending the evening with Dinah Hart had been one of the most pleasant experiences he'd had in months. He'd asked her over partly to get a rise out of her—sure she'd come to his store for more reasons than to ask him about saddles.

Her saying yes had been a nice surprise, their camaraderie even more so. Dinah had set the table while he'd grilled the chicken. Then she'd opened her bag of lettuce while he microwaved potatoes.

And though she looked at him curiously when he pulled out a pitcher of iced tea, she poured them two glasses. She'd even looked relieved, saying she couldn't drink anyway since Duke was away for the weekend and she was essentially running a one-woman show in the sheriff's office.

They'd talked about Leah and Colt, and Flynn and Ace. He'd told her about Cheyenne, and how she was living with their dad and slowly pulling out of her grief from losing her husband way too young. She grinned with him when he spoke about her twin girls, Sadie and Sammie.

Next they talked about Duke and Beau, and Beau's chances in the latest bull-riding competitions.

From there, it was only natural to talk about Tuf Hart, Dinah's younger brother. Austin's heart had gone out to her when she'd talked about how Tuf still hadn't shown up after getting out of the marines.

Family talk had eased into work, and she'd seemed genuinely interested in his shop. That worked out real nice, because he was genuinely interested in pretty much everything about her.

All too soon, it was almost midnight and she was getting to her feet. "Thanks, Austin. I…I really enjoyed myself."

"You're welcome. I liked having you here." For a moment, he let himself stare at her lips, remembering with sudden clarity what kissing her had been like.

Those lips parted, just as if she had read his mind.

Right there and then, he knew if he leaned forward she wouldn't be offended if he kissed her.

And he wanted to.

But it wasn't the right time. He was an emotionally toxic mess. Especially since he hadn't had the nerve to go to an AA meeting yet. Lord, he was needier than a newborn foal.

"So…good night, Dinah."

She blinked. "Oh. Sure. Good night." She looked a little hurt, as though he'd rejected her. Obviously she'd thought he was going to shorten that space between them and finally renew what had been floating between them for months.

He was still reluctant to see her go. "Any chance you going to church tomorrow?"

"I don't know. I don't go all that often. Why?"

"I'll be there. Thought if you were going to be there, too, maybe we could have lunch together after."

"You want to share another meal?"

She'd spouted the question as if he'd just asked to get in her pants. He bit the inside of his lip so he wouldn't smile. "Don't worry, I'm not trying to ruin your stash of Lean Cuisine dinners. I was thinking maybe we could get lunch at the Number 1 after. My treat."

After a fresh burst of interest, she looked more than a little hesitant. One of her hands flew to her hair, curling one of the wayward locks around her ear. "Maybe. I'll see what's going on in the office tomorrow."

"Fair enough. If I see you in church, I'll see you. Night, Dinah."

He stood at the door and watched her walk to her car, unlock it and finally drive away. He told himself he was just being a gentleman. After all, the sheriff probably didn't need a man looking after her.

He couldn't help but think maybe *Dinah* needed a man looking out for her. It was a real shame he wasn't the best candidate for the job.

DINAH HADN'T INTENDED to go to church. But when she called her mom, she sounded beyond pleased at the thought of Dinah sitting in the pew beside her. "We've had so many changes going on with the family lately, Dinah. It's good to take some time to give thanks, don't you think?"

There had only been one right answer. "Yes, ma'am."

So that was how she ended up sitting in church on Sunday, and in a dress, no less. She fingered the cotton fabric of her loose-fitting chambray blue dress. She'd paired it with boots and a concho belt. As dresses went, it was fairly casual. But it was a whole different look from her usual jeans and tan sheriff's shirt.

"You look so pretty, Dinah. So feminine! You should wear dresses more often, honey."

Her mother's voice had carried. A few seats over, Flynn chuckled. Ace winked. And then there was Austin, looking way too fine in pressed jeans and a white shirt so starched and bright it looked almost blinding.

But it didn't match the almost dazzling smile that deepened when he caught her eye.

Oh! Resolutely, she turned back around and concentrated on listening to the pastor. And not fussing with the fabric of her dress.

But though the pastor's message was a good one, Dinah felt her mind drift. She started thinking about work and filing and to-do lists. And about missing tack and one black stallion that was AWOL.

She began checking her watch every couple of minutes.

When the service ended and they were all filing out, her mother turned to her with a smile. "You coming back to the ranch, honey?"

"No, I should probably stay in town. Duke and Angie are away, you know."

"I know, but Beau will be there. As will Ace and Flynn. Colt and Leah are coming over, too. He's got news of Evan."

Dinah knew her brother was doing everything he could to forge a bond with his twelve-year-old son. Until very recently, Colt had thought Evan's mom had hoped he would keep his distance. But Colt marrying Leah had changed all that. Now he and the boy tried to spend time together every few weeks.

"I've got to work, Mom. The town elected me to be around."

"But it's Sunday."

"That doesn't matter." She softened her words with a smile. "I'm sorry. I'll try to come over later this week."

"All right."

Moments after waving off her mother, she practically ran into Austin. He was standing against the wall, with his arms crossed over his chest. Watching her.

Waiting for her.

Well, she certainly couldn't take him up on lunch at the Number 1 when she'd refused her mother. "Hey," she said.

"Dinah." His grin widened. "You look as pretty as a picture today."

This darn dress! "Thank you."

"Ready to go to lunch?"

"I'm sorry, I can't have lunch with you."

"Because?"

"Because I need to work. And I already refused my mother's invitation." And starting up something with Austin was such a very bad idea. She waited pensively, half-afraid he was going to try to talk her out of her decision.

But instead, he pushed away from the wall. "No problem. But don't forget to eat, okay?"

"I am sorry."

"It's no biggie. I'll be seeing you, D."

Now she was the one standing in the church's courtyard watching him.

But that wouldn't do. She needed to keep to herself and keep on alert. Just in case someone needed her.

Just in case.

WHEN JACK STILL HADN'T returned his call, Austin had decided to reach out to yet another person who'd tried to help him recently—Vanessa Anderson. Vanessa was now a nurse at the small family-practice doctor's office. She was also one of Austin's oldest friends. He'd taken a chance and called her just two hours ago. To his surprise, she'd answered right away and even coaxed him into coming in.

He'd readily agreed, though the knot in his stomach and the tremors in his hands revealed that it wasn't easy for him. To his shame, he was still too chicken to go to an AA meeting. There was something about standing up and admitting his problems to a bunch of strangers that scared the shit out of him.

But he had now gone six whole days without a drop to drink. And that was about six days longer than he could remember ever abstaining in years. It hadn't been easy. He'd felt a little shaky…and more than a little sick.

But he'd held firm.

So though he wasn't quite man enough to tell strangers about his problems, he'd decided to take Vanessa up on her offer. He and Vanessa Anderson had known each other forever and had always been firm friends, not lovers.

In addition, he'd heard rumors that she, too, had had to deal with some demons in her past.

"Austin, you did the right thing," Vanessa said as she sat down on the other vacant chair in the examining room of the doctor's office. "Asking for help is never easy. Some would say it's the most difficult thing to ever do."

Though Vanessa's heart was in the right place, Austin wasn't the least bit reassured by her remarks. In his book, a man should be better than his addictions. And so far, he'd done nothing but give in to his weaknesses at every turn.

"I'm just trying to get on with my life," he said through clenched teeth. "That's all."

"So…there's a meeting tonight. At seven o'clock at church. You going?"

"I'm thinking about it." Already his palms were sweating at the thought of going. What would they make him do? Tell his whole life story, which was nothing all that bad?

Make him admit over and over that he was an idiot?

And what if he saw people there he knew? His reputation as a Wright wasn't all that great in the first place. What was going to happen once everyone got a load of his latest batch of problems?

She gripped his shoulder and squeezed lightly. "It's going to be okay, Austin. Look, this is what I'm going to do. I'm going to give you a tetanus booster, and then I'm going to make sure you have my cell-phone number. It's sheer luck that I picked up my home line yesterday afternoon. I want you to promise me that you'll call my cell if you ever want to talk about the meetings. Or anything."

She wasn't making a pass at him. She wasn't treating his problem like a personal failure or like he should have been tougher than a bottle of Jim Beam.

Instead, she was offering him a hand. And that hand was so tempting but also so hard to accept, he could hardly look at her. "I don't know if I can actually go in that room, Van."

"Then don't think. Just go." She paused. "And if you find you're sitting in your truck, trying to find the will to open your door, call me. I'll talk you through it."

Offers like that didn't come easily. "Wow. I appreciate it, Vanessa."

"Hey, now. There's no need to turn bashful on me, Austin. I've been where you are. I promise you that."

"I still can't believe you were hooked on painkillers. I never knew until you told me."

"That's because I got help. It wasn't easy, but I did it." Her eyes shone as she continued. "I promise, there's a whole life for you on the other side, Austin. You've just got to make the choice to change. We both know that not everyone does."

He blinked, wondering if she was referring to his father. But even if she was, he let it slide. It was what it was—and he kind of figured there was little he could do about his father anyway. Thirty-plus years of being a disappointment pretty much cemented a man's reputation.

Putting on his hat, he nodded to Van. "Thanks for the shot and the ear. I was feeling like I had to move forward or I was never going to do a thing."

"Like I said, I've been there." Her gaze softened as she walked with him to the front door. The waiting room was vacant, and after he opened the glass door, she leaned into the opening slightly. The warm sun illuminated her skin just a little more, making her somewhat ordinary looks seem all of a sudden striking.

Before he thought how it might look, he wrapped her in a loose embrace and kissed her forehead. "I owe you, honey. Thank you."

"You don't owe me for this, Austin," she said. Her smile widened, and then she looked thoughtful as she glanced beyond him. "I think I should let you be going," she said cryptically as she went back inside.

Austin turned around to catch who'd caught her eye.

Then felt as if he'd just fallen over a cliff. "Hey, Dinah."

She was looking him over as though he was no better than an old Coke can that someone had tossed out the back window of their Chevy.

"Making the rounds this morning?"

Her voice was as sweet as corn syrup left out on the counter too long. It was obvious she'd misread his hug with Vanessa. Well, if she had, he was glad of that. The last thing he wanted was for anyone to know that he'd been at the clinic for testing and rehab advice.

"I'm getting a couple of things done. You?"

"I'm doing the same." Hazel eyes skimmed over him again as she tucked in her tan shirt a little more securely into the waistband of her jeans. "Just, you know…making the rounds, too." She coughed. "But for me, it's work."

"It's always work, right?"

She pursed her lips before answering. "Duke was out of town yesterday. I couldn't go out to lunch."

"You told me." Austin smiled. He couldn't help it. He liked putting her on the spot, just a little bit. Besides, she was cute. He knew to most people, Sheriff Hart was about the least "cute" woman in town.

A lot of the older men in Roundup didn't really trust a woman sheriff. They kept waiting for her to mess up. Added to the fact that a number of ranches in the vicinity were on alert because of the recent thefts in the area, and the fact that the Harts' fancy bucking horse was still missing? Well, a lot of people were just socking it all away as ammunition for the next election.

Others only saw Dinah as a Hart. Part of the rodeo royalty in the area. Though they didn't have bunches of money, their reputation was as good as gold. They won buckles, they had honor and they were fearless.

They also stuck together like a school of fish. Their ranks were solid and next to impossible to break. So even though he was a Wright—which meant he had a snowball's chance in hell to ever date her seriously—he couldn't resist pretending he had a shot with her. "I'm about to go down to the market and grab a couple of sandwiches and eat on the park bench. Want to join me?"

"It's kind of early for lunch."

"I know. But I've been up for hours. And I'd rather eat outside instead of in the store." Since she looked interested but just as skittish as a new foal…he kept talking. "Dinah, I know you've got to be prepared for just about anything…but I figure if you're in the town square, you'll be able to swoop down and stop any jaywalkers that might come upon us."

"I do more than stop jaywalkers."

"I know. I'm also starting to get the feeling you don't eat all that much."

"I have Snickers bars."

"Maybe you should supplement your candy-bar diet with some turkey every now and then." Her eyes widened with surprise. "Just saying."

"Austin—"

"Yeah?" He braced himself as he waited for a perfect freeze-out.

But instead of that, she nodded. "Sure. I mean, why not?"

Deciding it would be best to not give her any more time to think about things, he said, "Listen, you go scope us out a seat. I'll be right back."

"Oh, no. I'm coming with you and ordering my own sandwich."

"You, Dinah Hart, are a bit of a control freak."

"I've been called worse."

He smiled, but his heart softened. There really was so much more to the woman than most knew.

DINAH WOULD HAVE NEVER imagined Austin Wright as a tuna-salad type of guy. Roast beef would have been her pick. Turkey, maybe. But tuna salad on whole wheat? It kind of struck her as funny.

But maybe that had more to do with her choice, the Italian Stallion on a hoagie. And of course, barbecue potato chips and a Coke to wash it down.

Austin looked amused as he watched her take her first unhealthy bite. "You're a regular heart attack waiting to happen, Dinah."

"Not usually. Usually I watch every little thing." Except for her stash of Snickers bars, of course. Those she kept on hand for easy access. And emergency purposes.

And whenever she got particularly stressed.

"I've got to keep in shape, you know. For the job."

Frank appreciation appeared in his eyes before he tamped it down. "You've done a good job with that shape, too."

Now she was embarrassed. "I wasn't fishing for a compliment."

"I would have given it to you no matter what." He shrugged. "And I'm not complimenting you as much as stating a fact." Looking mildly uncomfortable himself, he took a good-size bite of his tuna and chewed.

"So, do you do this often?"

He shrugged. "I like being outside. I like the diner, too, but sometimes this is easier. And cheaper."

"More of a tuna guy." She tried hard, but the smile she was fighting still slipped out.

"I like fish. And the deli uses low-fat mayonnaise for me."

Because no one else was around, she let herself giggle. Just a little bit.

Austin's gaze warmed. "So you do laugh. I've been wondering."

"What's that supposed to mean?"

"About what you'd imagine it does. Usually, I only see you with your game face on."

It was tempting to pretend she didn't know what he was talking about, but she did. "I have to be serious when I'm on the job."

"And other times?"

"And other times," she agreed. "Getting reelected is important to me. Keeping everyone's respect is important to me, too. I don't want Duke to ever regret working with me. And I especially don't want the citizens to change their mind." Already full, she pushed the second half of her sandwich to one side.

"I don't think that's going to happen anytime soon. Everyone knows that Duke thinks you're doing a good job. Other folks think so, too."

"They might not think that way much longer," Dinah admitted. "A lot of people are real upset about the string of robberies, and I don't blame them. Money's tight right now, and folks are having to put out more money for better security systems and lighting. Some outfits have even had to hire on extra hands to help with patrols. Though everyone knows we've got a police force of two and a big area to patrol, that doesn't always count for much when the bills come in at the end of the month. Plus, people are still missing their tack."

"I hear you."

She lowered her voice. "Sometimes I worry that even my family is losing their faith in me."

"I seriously doubt that."

She appreciated the trust, but Dinah knew the truth of the matter. "Midnight's disappearance has stressed out just about everyone, especially my mom. If we can't track that horse down real soon, I worry that my mom is going to sell the ranch."

Austin shook his head in that confident way of his. "Ace wouldn't let that happen. Thunder Ranch is y'all's legacy." Eyeing her wrapped-up sandwich, he said, "Think you can eat another two bites?"

"You sound like my mother!"

"Naw, just trying to look out for you. Eat another bite, D."

Before she knew it, she was unwrapping the sandwich and taking one more bite. Just to please him.

His eyes lit up, looking pleased with himself. And that made her more than a little uncomfortable.

Quickly, she swallowed and got back on track with their conversation. "I know that Ace's judgment is good, and most times I don't mind following his directives. But all of us agree that no home is worth our mother's health."

"Dinah, I hear what you're saying, but I've got to tell you— you look like you're almost causing the end of the earth. Surely your family isn't blaming you for the flurry of thefts in the area. And what happened with Midnight is a crying shame. But if someone had really wanted that horse, then it stands to reason he took it far away. For all we know, that horse could be on the other side of the country by now."

Though she didn't like hearing his hypothesis, she appreciated his faith in her. It seemed she spent most of her life keeping up a Teflon front—pretending she was impervious to criticism. "No one in my family has come out to blame me.

Not in so many words. But I do know that they'd hoped I'd be better at my job…" Her voice drifted off as she recalled their last meal together.

Sitting at the big oak table, surrounded by everyone who knew and loved her, she could feel their frustration as if it was a tangible thing. It had been that way for weeks, too. The tension was getting so intense she knew it was just a matter of time before one of her brothers or cousins snapped. And the thing of it was that she wasn't even going to be able to blame them. Obviously she'd done a bad job with the investigation. Though she didn't know what she would have done differently, she was sure there had to have been a better way to get the answers.

"You okay?"

She started, realizing Austin had been staring at her while she'd been gazing off into nothing. "Sorry, I got caught up remembering something. But that moment of silence was probably a nice break from all of my whining."

His blue eyes sparkled. "You don't whine, Dinah. All you're doing is venting, and I promise, you don't have the cornerstone on that. Everyone needs to let things out every now and then."

"Maybe you're right. But between the horse missing and saddles getting stolen and high school kids acting up…and Duke only working part-time, I'm feeling like I don't have enough hours in the day to do it all."

Of course, the moment she spouted off her laundry list of complaints, she wished she could take it all back. What was she thinking? Austin could be working with the thieves!

After swallowing another bite, Austin kicked his legs out. Looking her over, he asked, "Do you mind if we don't talk about work for a bit?"

She jumped at his change in topic. "What do you want to talk about? Is something wrong? Do you need my help?"

His lips curved. "See, Dinah, that's your problem. You hardly know what else to do besides work."

Maybe he was right. Or maybe…she just wasn't sure what else to talk to him about. Sitting next to Austin made her pulse race a little faster and the rest of her feel suddenly feminine, as if she was still a woman even though she was the sheriff.

And here she'd been talking nonstop about herself. How self-absorbed could one woman be? "So, how is your shop doing?"

"I'm not going to talk to you about my store. That's work, too. You're just going to have to think of something far more interesting."

The jibe was given kindly, not mean-spirited at all. But it did serve to remind her that she had little else in her life besides her job.

Shoot, she couldn't even seem to give up a Sunday.

In defense, she said, "Austin, I'm not like all the other women you date."

The smiled vanished. "What the heck is that supposed to mean?"

She could have cursed her tongue. Now he was probably going to ask why she'd even brought up the other women. And then she was going to have to admit that she hadn't been able to get the picture of Austin hugging Vanessa out of her mind.

But since she'd started, she continued on. "I'm just saying there's more to me than just being a good-time girl with a lot of great hair."

"Hey, now. Hair?"

"I'm just saying that Vanessa sure has a lot of hair for being a nurse in a medical practice."

He sat up straighter. "Wait a minute. You're talking about Vanessa Anderson?"

"Yes, though I bet you know plenty of Vanessas." Now that it was all out in the open, she felt worse than catty. But how could she backtrack without seeming like more of a fool? "You know what I'm talking about, Austin," she said with a whole lot of bravado. "Vanessa must have more hair spray in that head of hair of hers than Miss Texas."

He scowled. "There's nothing wrong with her hairdo. She's got pretty hair." She knew that. That was the problem. "And, she's got a good brain and a good heart, too. She's a nurse, Dinah. And she's married!"

"She's a real pretty nurse. So, did she check you out?"

Stuffing the remainder of his sandwich in his plastic grocery sack, he glared hard at her. "Jeez, Dinah. I never thought you were the type of person who went around stereotyping others. Especially not other women, and especially not on a whim, just to be mean."

Did Austin Wright just say *whim?* "I don't stereotype."

He got to his feet. "I think you must. You're talking about Van like she's got nothing for nothing just because she's a beautiful woman who's embraced her share of the Walmart beauty aisle."

"I saw you hugging her." Even as the words spewed out of her mouth, she felt ten times as foolish. And suspiciously like a stalker.

"I was thanking her."

"For giving you a shot?" The moment her question left her mouth, she ached to take it back.

"I was thanking her for a lot of things, not that it's any of your business."

Dinah folded her arms over her chest. "I bet everything between you two was all business, all right."

"You don't know a thing." A muscle in his jaw twitched as he chose his words. "I think you're a real fine policewoman, Dinah, but at the moment, I'm thinking you've got a real prejudice toward me. And for the record, I just want to say that I'm plumb tired of it."

His words, and the unspoken hurt that lay behind them, made her cheeks flush. "I don't—"

"I think you've gone out of your way to give me more than a wide berth because of who my father is. And because of our past."

She felt more than a little sucker punched. "That's not true. I went over to your place for dinner on Saturday night."

"You know that was a fluke. Usually you avoid me like the plague."

"I—I don't..." she sputtered. It was a whole lot easier to call him a liar than to admit he was right.

"I think it might be truer than you want to admit."

Because she had eagerly hoisted an empty brain on Vanessa so she wouldn't have to look at her own insecurities, Dinah fended off his words by holding up her sandwich. "I don't think there's a reason in the world for us to continue this conversation. To make it easy for you, I'm going to stay right here and eat this while you move on."

Looking down at her, his too-handsome features were marred as he scowled. "Don't worry, Sheriff Hart. I won't make a point of sharing a bench with you anytime soon."

Wisely, she kept her mouth shut as he sauntered off. But boy, howdy! What was it with him and her reaction to him? All he had to do was be within breathing distance and she turned into some kind of high-strung, nagging witch who made petty comments about other girls in town.

That definitely wasn't her.

Gazing at her sandwich, she did what she usually did best. She analyzed things. Maybe her problems with Austin stemmed from the memories he triggered?

His wild ways made her remember too much. The way she used to run around without half a care in the world and a chip on her shoulder. She'd made mistakes, some in an inebriated fog that had made it almost impossible to recall them in detail.

Now when she looked at Austin or heard about his escapades, it brought back all those memories. Including the way she'd once plastered herself to him in a kiss that was so hot it could have set their clothes on fire. Even the memory of it made her ache with embarrassment all over again.

Now so glad she hadn't eaten more than she did, she wadded up her napkin and she tried that excuse on for size. Was that really the root of her problem? Austin merely brought back memories?

Chewing, she thought about it some more and tried to convince herself of that fact.

And then realized that while a person could fool a lot of people some of the time, it was near impossible to fool yourself.

Not more than once, anyway. Tossing the rest of her sandwich in the trash, she stomped to her office, checked her emails, then two hours later got into her cruiser and headed back over to the high school.

When they visited before, she'd been pleased to realize that Mrs. Marks had been willing to accept Dinah's suggestions for getting some of the kids back on track. They'd both agreed that getting to know the kids better was key, so she was going to visit a couple of classrooms.

Dinah had a feeling getting the kids to trust her was going to be something of a challenge. After all, when she had been in high school, the last thing in the world she would've wanted to do was visit with a sheriff.

Suddenly, she remembered what Flynn had said about those puppies of Angie's. Picking up her cell, she called Angie and asked if she could borrow a couple of the stray pups for a few hours.

She could use the puppies as a reason to talk to the kids. Talk to them about the dangers of dropping off stray animals.

A lot of people would go out of their way to avoid the sheriff. But a pair of cute, cuddly puppies?

Now, that was a whole other story.

Chapter Six

His first Alcoholics Anonymous meeting was in a smallish Sunday school classroom in the back of the church. Austin strode in with five minutes to spare and feeling more nervous than the moment when the chute flew open and he was sitting bareback on a horse with an attitude.

Could he do this? Everything inside of him was screaming no, he could not. But his head seemed to be in control for once and kept him firmly in tow. The entrance area was empty. The only sign of recent life was a neat rectangular-shaped whiteboard. On it, the daily schedule listed a whole slew of meetings and coordinating rooms.

Nowhere could he find a listing for the AA meeting.

Flummoxed, he pulled the sheet of paper where he'd written the meeting's date, time and place. Yep, he was in the right place at the right time on the right day.

Deciding to go another route, he glanced at the times. At seven o'clock, there was a meeting for Friends of Bill W. in Room 11. Vaguely he recalled hearing that was the code for the meeting.

Seeing shadows approaching on the sidewalk, he knew it was time to make a move. He could either walk down to the meeting, or he could make up a bunch of lies to the people who entered, and to himself. He'd definitely lied about his goals and intents before.

But then he remembered Dinah and the way she'd trotted off in a huff. He recalled the disdain he was sure he'd spotted in her holier-than-thou hazel eyes.

Finally he remembered that he'd woken up not too long ago with a phone call from a woman he didn't recall talking about events he didn't remember. If he didn't change his ways soon, he knew there was a good chance that the next phone call he got wasn't going to be as kind, and that the events were going to be a lot different than being rowdy and disgusting at a local bar.

That fear was enough to propel him down the hall. Door 11 was open and there were seven or eight men and women either talking or sitting quietly. He paused at the doorway, suddenly feeling as if he was back in Sunday school.

A man a good ten years older than him looked his way and paused. "Hi. I'm Alan. Are you here for our meeting?"

"I'm not entirely sure." He lowered his voice. "I'm here for an AA meeting?" Oh, he hated how he sounded. Like a squeaky, nervous kid.

The way he sounded years ago when he and Cheyenne went to visit his dad in prison.

But if Alan thought he was a weak-willed wuss, he didn't act like it. Instead he nodded in a relaxed, easygoing way. As though Austin had asked if he thought it might rain. "You're in the right spot. First meeting?"

"Yep." As if it wasn't obvious.

"I'm glad you came. You made the right decision."

Gathering more courage than it had ever taken him to climb on the back of a temperamental bronc, he said, "We'll see about that." Already he was thinking about exiting out of there quickly.

"No one's going to make you say a word." Alan smiled encouragingly. "But you can talk if you want to."

"I think I'll just do the watch-and-listen thing."

"Good enough." He stepped backward and let Austin walk on in.

He hesitated, then continued forward. Hoping all the while that he would learn the secret to sobriety. 'Cause he was already so nervous, his mouth was near parched. And the only thing that sounded as if it could quench his thirst involved Kentucky Bourbon.

There were chairs set up in a circle. Too ashamed to see anyone he knew, he took a chair in the middle of three empty ones, then immediately regretted his decision. Did sitting by himself make him stand out even more?

But just as he was cursing himself to hell, a middle-aged woman sat beside him. She had salt-and-pepper hair and her figure had thickened a little bit. She wore sensible shoes. But she smelled clean and pretty. Like a mom was supposed to.

That made him realize that it had been a long time since he'd thought about a mom or even missing his own.

He was still lost in that depressing train of thought when Alan walked to one of the chairs, stood in front of it and spoke. "Welcome, everyone," he said. "I hope you all had a good week."

To Austin's surprise, a guy three chairs down from him spoke up. "I almost didn't. I pulled out a Bud from my fridge and stared at it a good two hours last night."

Austin looked around, half waiting for everyone to either chide the guy for even having a bottle of beer at home…or haze him because he couldn't even handle one drink.

But instead, the atmosphere felt accepting, supportive. It was such a surprise, so different from the way most judgmental folks responded, that Austin felt himself relax.

And start listening a little harder.

"Did you open the bottle?" Alan asked.

"No. I was about to, then I pulled out my journal instead."

"Journal?" Austin blurted before he reminded himself that he was going to stay mute.

"Yeah," the kid said. Austin now realized the guy couldn't be much older than a teenager just out of high school. Pointing to the lady next to Austin, he added, "A couple of months ago, she talked about how writing about feelings had helped her. I started doing it, too. It helps."

The blonde lady smiled gently. "I'm real glad."

After a few seconds, the kid said, "I ended up putting that bottle back in the refrigerator." Then he smiled proudly. As if he'd just lasted eight seconds on a bull in the ring.

A couple of the people there clapped. One said, "Good for you."

Maybe it was because he didn't know if he could've poured out that beer. Maybe it was because he was a cocky son of a gun who always had to get himself in trouble.

Whatever the reason, Austin asked another question. "Why didn't you just pour it out?" If the kid was working that hard, it stood to reason that getting rid of the temptation was the best course of action.

"The beer was my dad's. He'd kill me if I poured it out." There was a whole lot unsaid, too. Like that his dad probably would've whipped his butt good if he'd drank it, too.

The boy's honesty hit Austin hard. He knew exactly what the kid meant. His father hadn't been one to share much when he'd been growing up, neither.

And he sure had never been the kind of man to accept another's weaknesses.

As Austin was telling himself to keep his expression neutral, to not let on how much what the kid said affected him, another person spoke. He told his story. Later two more spoke, talking about the difficulties of their jobs. One was even a teacher.

And then Alan stood up and started talking. Without a

stick of embarrassment, he told a story about how his girl-friend had called the sheriff's office on him years ago because she'd been afraid he was going to hurt her. Austin found himself only concentrating on the man's story, forgetting about himself, forgetting to care about what others thought of him.

Then the next thing he knew, everyone was saying a prayer and standing up.

Austin braced his elbows on his knees, looking down at his feet. Too embarrassed to walk out with everyone. Then only he and Alan remained.

"You did it," Alan said. "You made it through your first meeting."

First. That was the key word there, now, wasn't it? Going once didn't count. Going time and again, even when times were good, was hard.

Feeling his knees creak, Austin got to his feet. "Yeah, I did."

"You okay?"

He thought about it. "Yeah." He didn't even try to hide the surprise in his voice. "This was different than I thought." He got up, intending to walk right out.

But Alan stopped him. "Different how?"

"I thought everyone was going to talk at me. Tell me I was an idiot. Make me talk. Instead…" His voice drifted off. Unsure of how to put the rest of his thoughts into words.

"Instead you found out that we've all been in the same place?"

"Yeah."

Alan looked at him a good long minute, then said, "Wait a sec."

Austin stood there watching as Alan thumbed through a notebook, found a blank index card and wrote a couple things down. "Here's my name and number. In case you need it. Or have questions."

Without looking at it, Austin folded the card in half and stuffed it in his back pocket. "Thanks."

They walked out the door, then paused as Alan turned off the lights and locked it. "Come back next week."

Austin started walking down the hall. Gathering up his courage, he said, "What do I do if I want to drink before then?"

"Call me."

"You?"

"Yeah. I'd like to be your sponsor, son," he said quietly. "I think we could work real well together."

"You think?" Of course, he wished yet again he could keep his fricking mouth closed. He sounded too hopeful.

But if Alan was starting to have doubts about him, he didn't let on. "I think," he said with a small smile. "And maybe try that journaling thing. It worked for me."

He walked away before Austin could say another thing. But then Austin realized that his craving for bourbon was tamped down. It still lingered, but he could ignore it now.

So maybe there wasn't another thing left to say.

Chapter Seven

It was a quiet night in Roundup. Taking advantage of the fact, Dinah drove down a couple of the main streets in the town, stopping every once in a while to talk to folks and kid with a couple of teenagers. Her visit to the school, two of Angie's puppies in tow, had proven fruitful.

Kids had gathered around her, anxious to cuddle the pups. And all of them had nodded in agreement when she talked about the dangers of abandoning animals. The nonthreatening subject had started quite a few conversations. The high school principal had been as sharp as Dinah had remembered and had a list of kids who were proving to be habitual troublemakers. Some of them had had a couple of scrapes with Duke and her, as well.

Dinah took some time to visit classrooms and chat with a couple of kids in the halls when classes were changing. She also made a point of making eye contact with a few of the kids on the list. By the looks of fear that met her, she suspected that the worst of the pranks would quickly become nonexistent. Getting a detention was a whole lot different from getting arrested.

Now she was taking some time to keep her eyes and ears peeled for any news about missing tack while shooting the breeze along Main Street. As far as she and Duke were concerned, it never hurt to reach out to folks in a positive way.

Around nine o'clock, she turned down Highway 12 and headed out to the ranch. Seeing the rolling hills dotted with familiar ponderosa pine and sandstone rock outcroppings always made her smile. Coming home always made her count her blessings. Thunder Ranch was a wonderful place to grow up.

Because she was constantly "on," being the newly elected official that she was, Dinah had made a promise to herself to come home and recharge more often. But those promises were weakened by the nagging sense that she was letting everyone in the family down by not solving the mystery surrounding the missing tack and Midnight, and as a result she'd stayed away too much.

It had been too long since she'd been home. She really did have a hankering for some downtime.

After driving over the cattle guard and down the well-maintained gravel road—known to all of them as Thunder Road—she glanced at the equestrian barn, the outside pens, and finally the pool and fire pit. At last she pulled up to the house on the left. The fieldstone walls glimmered against her cruiser's headlights, catching her attention, practically daring her to look anywhere else.

Whimsically, she thought the walls were guiding her toward home. The moment she parked, Sarah Hart opened the back kitchen door and hurried outside. Over her loose jeans and white button-down, she wore her usual soft brown corduroy jacket. Though they'd all offered to buy her something a little snazzier and warmer, her mother had always refused the offer.

Dinah had a feeling the jacket gave her mom a sense of comfort that went beyond simple warmth.

"Dinah, I didn't expect to see you so soon. Is anything wrong?"

Her mother's worried expression shamed Dinah. Wow, she

really had become a scarce visitor! It seemed her mother now thought she would only come by when she needed something.

"Nothing's wrong, Mom. I just thought I'd stop by and see how you were doing."

"Sure?" Her mom's blue eyes looked her over, top to bottom. The scan as thorough as an airport screener.

Dinah clasped her mother's arm, the worn corduroy feeling as soft and comfortable as one of her mother's hugs. "I promise. Now, how are you?"

Satisfied that her daughter was fine, her mother's tough outer shell seemed to crack a bit. "Oh, I'm all right."

"Mom, what is it now?" Immediately, she regretted her choice of words. Yet again, her clumsy questioning showed that she hadn't let loose or come home nearly often enough. Here she was greeting her mother as though she was in the middle of an interrogation.

Plus, there were so many things that could be wrong, her mother probably had to do a mental toss to determine which problem she wanted to focus on. Tempering her tone, she asked, "Are you still worried about Midnight? I promise you, Duke and I are doing everything possible to locate that horse."

She took a breath, ready to describe the internet blog and the Missing posters and her communications with neighboring law-enforcement agencies.

"Honey, I know that." Her mother shrugged, her eyes tearing up. "It's nothing. I was just sitting here thinking about Tuf. And missing your dad tonight. Then, here you are. And sometimes seeing you…" She let the words slide.

But Dinah couldn't let it go. "Seeing me?"

"You have some of the same mannerisms as your father." Looking at her fondly, her mother laughed. "When you jut out your chin like you do when you're trying to prove a point, I'd swear John was right here in spirit."

Dinah was struck dumb. She had adored her father. But

when they'd discovered just how much he'd been drinking... and just what a mess he'd left the ranch in...well, it wedged a deep scar inside of her.

Whether on purpose or not, she'd been attempting to distance herself from him. Because she seemed to only remember his flaws. But doing that also meant she had distanced herself from his good points, too.

"I'm sorry you're missing Dad tonight." Dinah didn't dare mention Tuf. All of them ached for her brother.

"I'm all right. Just being honest." Wrapping an arm around Dinah's shoulders, she ushered her into the kitchen.

The warm terra-cotta colors of the tile floor and kitchen counters eased nerves she didn't even know had been frayed. The familiar space, combined with the tantalizing smell of fresh-baked bread and beef-barley soup and her mother's matter-of-fact way of speaking, completed the journey home. Suddenly a lump had formed in her throat, and she wasn't even sure where it had come from.

Seeking to lighten the mood, she cleared her throat and intentionally brightened her voice. "Looks like you've been baking, Mom."

"A little. Just some bread. Rosemary wheat."

Hot fresh bread, seasoned with herbs grown from her mother's herb garden, made her mouth water. No one cooked like her mother. No one. She hadn't planned to eat any more, but suddenly the comforts of home overran any worries about her weight. "Got any left?"

"For you I do." Her mom glanced at her sideways for a moment before pulling out a mug and a bowl, too. "I've got a feeling you haven't eaten supper. Have you?"

"No, ma'am."

"Would you like some soup? I made beef barley this afternoon."

Getting to her feet, she stepped toward the row of cabinets next to the stove. "That sounds great. I'll help."

"No, miss. You sit. I'll serve it up."

"Mom, you don't have to wait on me."

"It's my house. My house, my serving."

Dinah knew she was joking. From the time her children had been small, they'd known better than to sit and watch their mother wait on them. "Mom, we need to watch your heart."

"My heart likes me walking around a bit. My heart also likes fussing over my daughter."

"But—"

"It's just soup, Dinah. Sit."

Her mother might be feeling melancholy, but she hadn't lost her ability to order her children around. "Yes, ma'am." As her mother ladled out the soup, Dinah looked around. "Where's Ace?"

"I think he and Flynn are at their own place, but he should be coming around any minute. He usually does stop by in the evening, at least for a little bit."

Dinah couldn't help but notice the wistful tone in her mother's voice, matched by the somewhat lonely words. Guilt hit Dinah again.

But while she'd been only thinking about herself and her faults, her brother had been taking up the slack. "I'm sorry I haven't been coming over here more often."

Her mother paused while pouring the coffee. "Dinah, I know you've been busy. I don't expect you to change your life for me."

"Everyone's busy. Colt is busy running the steers and bucking operation, and riding in rodeos. Ace is managing things and working hard in his practice. They're both married, Colt has kids, but they still come over here a lot. I've got no excuse."

"They work here."

"I know. But still…"

"We all have time to work and rest, Dinah. All you can do is do the best you can." There was a sharpness in her mother's tone—signaling to Dinah she'd better stop complaining. "Now, eat up."

Obediently, she dug in. The warm goodness of the homemade soup tasted just as delicious as it always did.

She smiled as she bit down on a piece of potato, then followed that with a bite of bread. "No one cooks like you do, Mom."

Hands circled around her own stoneware coffee cup, her mother laughed. "I reckon kids have been saying that to their mothers for a hundred years."

"Maybe you're right. So, tell me what's been going on."

Her mother was only too glad to fill her in on Angie and Luke, and Ace and Flynn, and Colt and Leah. The conversation next turned to horses and rodeo standings and plans for the future. Dinah listened as she spooned every last drop of soup into her mouth.

When she was done, her mother smiled. "Remind me to send some food home with you. You're obviously not eating much."

She was tempted to refuse, but accepted gratefully instead. "Thanks."

"Now tell me what you've been up to today."

"Work. Trying to figure out what's been going on with all the stolen tack."

"Any new leads?"

She ached to say that she did have leads. But of course she and Duke had squat. "Nothing new. But I'm trying, and Duke has reached out to just about everybody in a hundred-mile radius. We're not going to give up, Mom. And we sure haven't given up on Midnight."

For the first time, her mother looked really worried. "I know you're trying your best." Running a hand through her silver hair, she said, "I tell you, I thought nothing could worry me more than when Colt wanted to let Midnight go back into the ring. Now I realize that was small potatoes. I'm truly worried about that horse." Her voice cracked. "He's already been through so much. Just thinking about someone abusing him makes my heart just about break."

Feeling guiltier than ever, Dinah stared at her empty soup bowl. "I know, Mom. I promise, if it's the last thing I do, I'll find that horse."

"I know that, honey. Don't mind me. I'm simply feeling a little maudlin tonight." After another sip of coffee, she said, "So, rumor has it you and Austin Wright were spotted out in the park."

Shoot. The last thing she needed was more talk about her and Austin. Some folks had nothing better to do than rehash old sparks—or to look for sparks or fireworks when there weren't any. "It was nothing. We just happened to be sharing some sandwiches."

"Is that right?" Slowly, her mother smiled. "I'm glad you and Austin have renewed your friendship. I've always had a soft spot for him myself."

"You've had a soft spot for Austin? Austin Wright? Really?" Dinah stared at her mother in shock. She'd always thought her mom didn't think too highly of Austin Wright or want her only daughter hanging around the likes of him.

And, like back then, her mother wasn't falling for her disclaimers for a minute. "Come, now, Dinah. You've got to admit that Austin always did have a certain charm."

He had a lot of things, that was true. A terrible reputation. Too-blue eyes. And a whole lot of missed opportunities. And dark hair that curled just the right way along the nape of his neck. "Charm might be all he has," she scoffed as the kitchen door opened.

Inside came Ace, her favorite brother, looking as tall and impressive as always. She'd always privately thought nothing could ever match her brother in much.

"Hey, Ace," she said.

If he noticed that she still lit up like a Christmas tree whenever he was around, he didn't let on. Instead he just smiled and pressed his lips to her head. "What's new?"

"Nothing." Lifting up her spoon, she stated the obvious. "Eating Mom's cooking."

He chuckled and smiled their mom's way. "That should be reason enough to stop by more often."

She flushed. Ace had a way with words, and that was a fact. In only ten words, he'd been able to compliment their mother, chide her absence and comment on her poor nutrition all at the same time.

But his jibe definitely had found a home, and it was all the reminder she needed to come by more often. "I agree," she mumbled. "Mom's cooking is better than anyone else's."

Her mother's cheeks bloomed, but she shooed off the fancy talk with a swish of a dishrag. "Ace, we were just talking about Austin Wright when you came in."

His gaze sharpened. "Oh, yeah? How is Austin doing, Dinah?"

"Oh, I don't know."

For once, her mother wasn't her defender. "I don't think that's quite true, Dinah. As a matter of fact, I think you know real well how Austin is doing."

Ace crossed his arms over his muscular chest. "Let's hear it, then. Tell me some news."

"It's nothing special. In fact, all I know is plenty I wish I didn't." For a moment, she considered tattling on the man, talking about his latest mess at the honky-tonk and her weak suspicions about his involvement in the thefts, but refrained. If she started down that path, she would be treading dangerously close to being unprofessional.

"Is that right? What do you know, Dinah?"

"Nothing. Ignore me. I'm just tired and spouting nonsense." She could feel her neck start to heat that very moment. Yes, she might be able to shoot her Glock with practiced ease, but talking boys around her brother showed she still had a whole lot of emotional maturing to do.

"Huh. I don't think that's it."

She looked at her eldest brother thoughtfully. "Now it sounds like you know something I don't. Spill."

After pouring himself a cup of coffee, Ace joined the two of them at the island table. "I don't know all that much. It's just that I've always thought there was more to Austin than anyone gave him credit for."

"Because of how he rode?" He could have been a real contender in the circuit if he'd wanted to go that route. In Sheridan, Duke told her that he won a good amount of money. Enough to get his old black truck fixed right, and with a little left over, too.

"Well, yeah. He is a fine bareback rider." He paused, sipping his coffee. "But I was really thinking more about how he grew up."

She knew quite a bit about Austin's family. But yet again, it sounded as if Ace knew more. "What about it?"

Glancing sideways at their mom, he said, "I can't imagine what it would be like to grow up in the shadow of a man nobody respects. A man who spent a couple of years in the state prison out near Deer Lodge. That would be real difficult, I think."

Her knee-jerk reaction was to push that off. She'd been in law enforcement long enough to know that a whole lot of folks didn't have the best home lives behind their closed doors. But that was unkind—and putting things too simply. A lot of people might not have the best home life, but they also were a long way from having a father who'd been to prison.

"I haven't heard much news about Buddy Wright lately. He must be keeping his head down."

"Or cleaning up his act," their mother said. "I heard that when Cheyenne came back with her girls, she put her foot down on Buddy's drinking."

Dinah didn't want to be unkind, but she kind of figured there was barely a snowball's chance in hell that Buddy Wright had decided to suddenly stop drinking and become a model citizen for his granddaughters. "Maybe. Time will tell, I guess."

A line formed between Ace's brows. "Dinah, I might be inclined to agree with you about Buddy, but Austin's a good man. He started that store out of next to nothing, and he's making a success of it. And while all of us have each other to depend on…he's had no one to speak of. Not until Cheyenne came back from California."

"Have you spoken to her lately?" their mother asked.

"I haven't." Dinah inwardly winced. Cheyenne was yet another of her friends she hadn't made much of an effort to get back in touch with since she'd been elected sheriff. That was a shame, too, since Cheyenne, Leah and she had had some great times when the three of them had been competing in barrel races.

Maybe it was the reminder that she wasn't quite the model of society that she was hoping to present to the public. Maybe all this talk of Austin's problems felt vaguely disloyal.

But whatever the reason, she got on her high horse. "You know, Austin's not quite the sorry, lonely man you make him out to be, Ace."

He lifted his hands and stepped backward. "Whoa, Dinah. What's up with you? A little touchy about him?"

"No, I'm trying to concentrate on the facts, not speculation."

"All right…since you're all into speaking like the law, and since you seem to know Austin real well right now, I'll let you have that one."

Now she was embarrassed. "I didn't say I knew him 'real well.'"

"Whatever. But I will ask you this. How would you have felt if not a one of us came to your graduation from the police academy? I've always thought it would be hard to go through life alone. Everyone needs something or someone to lean on."

Even the thought of one of the most important days of her life passing without their support took her breath away. They'd had her back every step of the way.

"You know I wouldn't be who I am without our family." It hurt to agree with him, but she couldn't deny his reasoning.

"And you would agree that family helps us all get through hard times?"

"Of course."

"Then let me ask you this. How do you think I'd feel if Flynn was constantly wondering if I was sneaking around, drinking and carousing?"

"I'm not doing that. And I'm the sheriff." She also wasn't Austin's wife!

"You're not thinking like a sheriff. You're thinking like a woman."

"Sometimes a woman has every right to be suspicious of the man in her life," she snapped. "Sometimes he has secrets."

Darting a glance at her mother, Dinah gasped. Her mother was pale, but to her surprise, she didn't refute Ace's words. Or ask that he honor their father's memory in a better way.

So she stood up for her father. "Ace, what you're bringing up, that's not fair."

"No. It sure as hell isn't. Gossip like that can be real hurtful, don't you think?" To her chagrin, Ace winked before pushing away from the table and standing up. "See you later, Mom. I'm gonna go get back to Flynn."

"Night, Ace," their mother said with a soft smile as he walked out the door.

Dinah, on the other hand, felt as though she'd been given a talking to.

She just wished she knew what she'd done wrong.

Chapter Eight

When the phone rang in the pitch-black comfort of her warm bed, Dinah knew there was only one person who could have been on the other side of the line.

"Duke, what happened?" she said wearily.

"Another robbery."

Sitting up and stifling a yawn, she glanced at the old-fashioned alarm clock on the side of the bed. "It's barely midnight." So far, the majority of the thefts had taken place in the early-morning hours.

"I know. It makes no sense…but there you go."

Most of the time, she loved Duke's quiet, no-nonsense way of laying everything out in the open. But tonight, bleary-eyed with sleep? It made her itch for a lead. "Okay. Give me the facts. When was it reported? Whose ranch?" Oh, please don't let it be her family's, she thought selfishly.

"It was the Emersons. They reckon several thousand dollars of saddles and bridles were stolen, including their daughter Janine's show saddle."

"Crap."

His voice deepened. "Dinah, I think we both need to show up for this one."

Dinah agreed. The Emerson ranch, Emerald Sky, was a top-of-the-line outfit at the edge of their jurisdiction. The owners, Curt and Kelly, were good people but a little high in the instep and a bit high-strung, too. They were definitely a family who was used to people bending down to their reputations.

Dinah felt sure that they would find a way to make the robbery the sheriff's responsibility—even if their cameras weren't working or if they had a new hand they hadn't checked out good.

"Want to come pick me up in ten?"

"Will you be ready in ten? Because, you know, I could give you fifteen minutes. It's not like the Emersons are going anywhere." His voice was laced with amusement.

Now that Duke was married, her normally shy cousin seemed to have a whole new awareness of the time it took a woman to primp. Even though Angie seemed to be strictly wash-and-wear, it was a fact that long hair and makeup took a little more time than splashing water over a face and throwing on a hat.

"Ten will be plenty."

"All right…"

Thinking about Mr. and Mrs. Emerson, and how she was going to need every bit of ammunition at her disposal to be at her best, she chuckled. "Actually, you'd better make it fifteen minutes, Duke. I think I better look as sharp as possible for our visit." And that, of course, meant that she needed to tame her curls into some kind of semblance of order.

"I'll slick back my hair, too."

She laughed as she hung up, then turned on her bedside lamp. Though it was true that she didn't primp all that much, she had a feeling most folks would be surprised to see her little set of rented rooms at the back of the old Victorian.

The walls were painted a slick eggshell, reminding her of fresh cream in the morning. Through mail-order catalogs, she'd ordered lace curtains and a thick quilt that was cream, too.

On the smooth wooden floor lay an old Oriental carpet done in shades of blue that she'd spied at a garage sale a couple of months ago. The blues and grays in the carpet were pretty much the only color in the room. Everything else was soothing and delicate.

Walking over to her dressing table, complete with a pewter colored lamp and an oval mirror, she hastily took a straightener to the worst of the curls and slipped on a sweater, jeans and a pair of recently polished boots. Once she was satisfied with that, she walked past the jumble of romance novels she kept meaning to organize and the two pairs of boots she kept meaning to put in her closet. Maybe one day she'd actually take the time to do those things.

Maybe one day she'd actually have some extra time!

Efficiently, she holstered her gun, slid on her uniform jacket and strode out the door, locked it securely behind her and went outside to wait for Duke.

So far, no one besides family had actually come inside her place. She'd liked it that way. The last thing she needed was for anyone to realize that she was a whole lot softer than people thought.

That could only get a lady sheriff into trouble.

As she'd feared, when she and Duke got to the Emerald Ranch, the whole gang was fired up and ready for blood. Wisely, Dinah sent Duke straight out to the barn to start questioning while she headed up to the main house.

It was an oversize Spanish-style hacienda with wide-planked wooden floors, priceless Western paintings and bronzes. The thick walls seemed to give a sense of quiet that had never been a part of Thunder Ranch.

Ava, their housekeeper, let her in and escorted her across the wide foyer, down a hall filled with framed and matted photographs of various Emerson men and women winning awards and buckles. At last, she entered a large living room with two ornate Oriental rugs at either end.

Mr. and Mrs. Emerson were sitting side by side on a tan leather couch and watched her approach.

Forcing herself to not slow her pace, she strode forward, hoping her purposeful stride covered up the nervousness she was feeling. "Hear you've had some trouble," she said in greeting. "I'm sure sorry about that."

Mr. Emerson stood up and shook her hand. "Dinah. Thank you for coming out here so quickly."

Dinah knew he wasn't calling her "Sheriff Hart" on purpose. Just a way to make sure that she knew her place. "Duke is already outside talking to your hands. Want to fill me in?"

Curt Emerson glanced at his wife, then shrugged as he took a seat and gestured for Dinah to sit down, as well. "Not much to say, Dinah. One of the hands buzzed me an hour ago from the equestrian barn, saying that the back door had been jimmied. Didn't take a whole lot of detective work to see that Janine's show saddle had been taken."

Unfortunately, the story sounded all too familiar. What also was familiar was the slow, raging burst of anger that threatened to blow her temper once and for all. She was sick and tired of being two steps behind the idiots.

She took out her pad of paper and pencil and wrote down the details. "I'm assuming your foreman has some photos of the saddle."

"He does. Insurance folks do, too." Frowning, Curt said, "It was hand-tooled leather, designed by Beau Adams himself."

Mrs. Emerson spoke for the first time. "When Curt first told me he wanted to catalog most of our belongings, I thought he was being a bit paranoid. But I guess you can't be too careful these days. It's a sign of the times."

Or a sign that their local sheriff couldn't get a break in the case, Dinah thought wryly. However, it would do no good to share that thought out loud. Instead, she kept her armor of confidence firmly wrapped around her as she stood up. "Yes, ma'am. Well, I think I'll go on out and see what Duke found out."

Mr. Emerson stood, as well. "It would mean a lot to me if you apprehended these thieves real soon, Sheriff. Folks around here have enough to deal with without having to beef up their security details." He paused. "You know, back when Babcock and Clark were talking about needing a man for your job, I thought they were just being jerks. But if things don't get better soon, I'd be tempted to listen to them."

"Yes, sir," she murmured, swallowing her pride. The men he spoke of had boys who had been burrs in the backside for her and Duke more than once. It had felt as if Rory Clark and Tracy Babcock were simply waiting for her and Duke to make a major mistake.

What no one seemed to remember, however, was that her family had also been targets of the thieves. In addition, they were missing their champion horse!

Not that anyone in the area really cared two sticks about that.

Keeping her game face on, she held out her hand to the couple. "It's going to take us a while to check for prints and collect evidence. If you need anything, please don't hesitate to ask."

"You just find that thief, Dinah. You can even string him up with our blessing." Mr. Emerson's smile was cordial, but his voice had a touch of iron in it.

With that command still ringing in her ears, she turned on her heel and ventured out to the barn—where she hoped Duke was having more luck.

He was—but his good news just about broke her heart, though she didn't even want to admit to herself why.

Duke's expression was grim as he waited for her to respond. "Though Pete said he thought it was Austin's truck, we both know that doesn't mean much," he said slowly. "Why, over the last few months, I've seen a dozen so-called eyewitness reports where everyone claimed they saw a different man or vehicle."

"I hear you, Duke. But if Pete says he saw an old Chevy truck that had a chrome bumper exactly like Austin Wright's, I'm going to have to check it out. Pete has no reason to lie that I know of." She'd also known Pete for years. She'd never known him to make things up.

"It's a crying shame, though. Austin would be about the last person in the world I'd want to see resort to stealing tack."

She felt the same way. Ace's words were still ringing in her ears, reminding her that Austin hadn't had an easy time of it. She wanted to give him the same benefit of the doubt that so many other people had given her. But while it was true that some people did grow and change, it was also a simple fact that others did not.

And what was also in Austin's corner, working against him almost every hour of the day, was that he came from a troubled home, with a parent who had served time in prison for stealing cattle. That couldn't ever be ignored.

"I'll talk to him in the morning."

Duke narrowed his eyes. "It's only midnight. It might be better if we went by right now."

"I don't think so. All that would do is put both him and me on the defensive. This isn't a kidnapping or even a horse-napping, right? It's merely a saddle theft."

"Damn expensive saddle theft. Janine Emerson's saddle was appraised for over eight grand." Duke scratched his head. "This has gone from bad to worse, Dinah. Every time we turn around, our no-good thieves seem to raise the stakes."

With the exception of Midnight, she agreed. It did seem as if the thieves were getting pretty darn expensive tastes.

After another hour or so, they headed home. Duke, to his sweet Angie.

Dinah? To a night of sleepless tossing and turning. Waiting for dawn. And waiting to question a man who had one time been a real good friend. And who she'd come very close to kissing just a few nights ago.

Now that things between them were bound to get worse, Dinah kind of wished she had.

Chapter Nine

The moment Dinah Hart sauntered into his shop, tan sheriff's shirt neatly tucked, hand lightly resting on the gun on her hip, expression solemn, Austin knew she had a bone to pick with him.

Though he could meet her somber expression easily, he didn't care to do that. Like always, he found it a heck of a lot easier to don his good-old-boy attitude and wear it proudly, with style. "Sheriff Hart, it's a pleasure to see you. What brings you in? Need a new pair of jeans, perchance?"

That—as he'd hoped—brought her up short. "I've never heard a man say 'perchance,' Austin."

"That's because I'm an individual. Some might even call me unique." He raised a brow. "Or haven't you heard?"

To his delight, he saw her lips twitch, signaling that somehow, someway, he'd broken through her serious facade. "I have heard that. Much to my shame."

He walked around the counter and made a show of looking her jeans over. As if she could ever not fill them out well. "So, what are you thinking? Size-four Wranglers? Or maybe something a little fancier?" He waggled his brows. "Or tighter?"

Smoothing her hands down a pair of very fine hips, Dinah looked more than a little taken aback. "I didn't know you had gotten so adept at sizing women and their jeans."

"It's been a lifelong project. It's taken a bit of practice, but my ability to guess a woman's clothing size is uncanny."

"I can only imagine the homework you had to do."

He sighed dramatically. "It was a difficult job, but it had to be done. For the sake of the store, of course."

"Of course," she echoed sarcastically. "I'm surprised the women you've practiced on haven't started a club…or a support group."

"Work always comes first, you know." Staring at her, he tried to figure out what was specifically different about her. She was upset about something, and it wasn't the usual. "You're not still fixated on Vanessa, are you?"

"No. I do owe you an apology for the way I sounded. I know you wouldn't fool around with a married woman. And Vanessa wouldn't act like that, either." Her cheeks flushing, she swallowed hard, then continued. "In addition, Vanessa's never been anything but nice to me, and Duke's wife, Angie, has even mentioned that she's been a sweetheart with her son, Luke. I can only blame my peevishness on being tired and stressed out."

"I'll take that." For a moment, he was tempted to run his hands over her shoulders. Plant a thumb under her collar and rub her smooth skin. Ease those muscles.

More than that, she looked as though she needed someone to believe in her. "You can't do it all, Dinah," he said quietly. "Believe me, I've tried."

Maybe it was the mention of being human. Maybe she thought he was insinuating that she was weak. But whatever the reason, her softness vanished as if it had been a figment of his imagination. "Austin, I didn't come in here to get outfitted. Or comforted. By you."

That "by you" pissed him off. "Why did you come in here, Dinah?"

Oh, that drawl. Oh, the way that starched blue shirt made

his eyes look so beautiful. Steeling herself, Dinah said, "I need to know what you were doing last night. And I need to ask you if I can take a look around the store."

"Excuse me?"

There was a part of her that completely got his irritation. Shoot, she would have been irritated, too. No one wanted to be a suspect, especially not on a trumped-up hunch that someone might have seen his old truck in the vicinity "sometime" around the time of the suspected robbery. Even if that witness had been Pete Boone.

"There was a robbery last night, Austin. I need to know where you were."

"Why?" His voice hardened. He folded his arms over his chest. "Are you thinking that I might have something to do with it?"

"I didn't say that." She rolled her shoulders. Though it sounded lame, she said, "Actually, I was kind of hoping we could talk through what you were doing last night."

"Talk through?"

"You know, as friends."

He cocked his head to one side. "Friends? I don't think so. I don't know what we are, but I think calling us 'friends' might be stretching the definition of our relationship."

His words stung. Even though they were true. She wanted to kiss him, that was true. But she didn't trust him. At all.

She didn't know what they had become, but the sad truth was that they'd long ago said goodbye to their former friendship.

Now it didn't matter what they were. "Austin, look, this is making me uncomfortable, too. But someone said that they might have seen your truck in the vicinity of a recent robbery. It's my duty to investigate every loose end."

"I wasn't out stealing tack on Monday night, Dinah."

"So where were you?"

Instead of answering, he lobbed another question her way. "Where was the robbery? Whose ranch?"

"I'm not going to tell you that." *Please,* she begged silently, *just tell me your story and let it have witnesses!*

"I'm not going to tell you where I was last night."

"Were you here?"

"Not all night."

"Who were you with? Can you give me her name?"

"'Her name'?" His expression became colder. "So you're assuming that I was with a woman...if I wasn't out gallivanting around the countryside stealing saddles."

Her heart suddenly felt as though it was about to jump out of her chest. "I didn't say that."

"It was close enough."

"Come on, Austin. Just tell me."

"No. Where I was isn't any of your business."

It made no sense, but she felt a fierce stab of jealousy coil through her. "If you were with a woman, I don't care. I promise, I won't embarrass her. I just need an alibi."

He bit his lip, looking torn and troubled and more than a little bit horrified, but he stuck to his guns. "I wasn't with a woman, Dinah. I'm not going to tell you where I was."

Obviously, they'd reached a standstill. She tried another tack. "I'm going to walk in the back and look around."

He shook his head. "I don't think so."

"Austin, don't be difficult," she snapped. Lord have mercy, why did the man have to argue and fuss about everything? If he'd only give her a straight answer every once in a blue moon, their relationship would be a whole lot smoother. "You and I both know that I'm trying to do my job."

But her offer of conciliatory conversation went over about as well as a deflated hot-air balloon. His scowl deepened and his voice dipped to a dangerous low. "As far as I'm concerned, I still have rights. Is that true?"

With extreme effort, she refrained from rolling her eyes. "Of course it is."

"Then I'm very sorry, ma'am, but if you really feel the need to search my store, you're going to have to go get yourself a warrant."

Getting a search warrant meant a heap of paperwork and a call to either a district attorney or a judge. It meant more bitter feelings and more time wasted.

It meant more time fussing and waiting instead of using her limited time to check out other leads.

Because, darn it, didn't he see that she was really trying to clear his name?

"Think about what you're saying."

His gaze lit on her like laser beams, practically scorching her with disdain. "Oh, I'm thinking about it. I'm thinking about how you've taken to waltzing in here, time after time, and always suspecting the worst of me. Fact is, I'm pretty darn sick of it."

"That's not fair, and it's not true." Though, maybe it kind of was? Ace seemed to think she was always jumping on the no-good-Wright bandwagon.

His blue eyes, which had always looked so dreamy on the rodeo circuit and perfectly warm in the sunlight in the park, looked icy cold and frosty now. "I completely agree with you. This doesn't feel fair at all. But someone real smart once told me that life wasn't fair."

"And your point is?"

"My point is that this inquisition of yours chaps me something fierce, Dinah Hart. I know you always considered me white trash. But I thought you at least thought I was the honest kind. If you want to pin a string of robberies on me, if you really think I'm capable of stealing from my friends and neighbors—and then being fool enough to sell the stock in my store—then you can go get yourself a damn search warrant and do it legally."

As she stood there, mouth open in shock, he turned away from her and walked right down the main aisle to his back storage room.

Feeling a bit like a girl getting jilted at the dance, she watched him leave.

And realized that while he was putting her down, he'd uncovered something she'd kept carefully hidden: after all this time, she still had a whole lot of feelings for Austin Wright.

And the realization came at the exact wrong time and the exact wrong place.

And he was right. Life wasn't fair. It wasn't fair at all.

"You just wait. I'm going to go get that damn warrant, Austin!" she called out. "And when I come back, you better be here." Cocking her head, she braced herself for his comeback.

But she heard nothing other than the frustrated silence of a man on the edge.

Pivoting on her heel, she stomped out, hoping she could find a judge to give her a search warrant in under twenty-four hours.

THE MOMENT HE HEARD THE FRONT door of the shop close, Austin rested his head against the wall of his makeshift office and counted to ten.

His hands were shaking, he was so frustrated with that woman. A sudden, sharp need for a shot of Maker's Mark hit him hard. Shoot, even a bottle of Bud would do the trick.

That's what he needed, what he craved. Just a few hours of comforting oblivion. Where he wouldn't have to think about his reputation or Dinah's suspicions…or the way he suddenly felt a hell of a lot like his dad.

Before he knew it, he'd grabbed his hat and his keys, ready

to lock up and spend the next few hours on a date with a bottle of bourbon.

Only the jangle of the door opening again saved him. "Austin? You in here?"

There was only one woman who had that husky, almost breathless voice. His sister, Cheyenne.

And he was so grateful, he almost kissed her. "Yeah," he said after a cough. "I'm in the office. I'll be right out."

"Don't bother, we'll come on back." She popped around the corner, her long auburn hair swinging around her shoulders with every sway of her hips. But the moment she took a good look at him, sitting on his chair behind his desk, her happy smile dimmed. "You look beat-up."

He knew she was talking about the strain on his face. Knowing how he looked, and knowing how much he hated the reason behind it, he tried to laugh it off. "That good, huh?"

Glancing over at Sadie and Sammie, he noticed that they were watching him with wary expressions. Not wanting to scare them, he smiled their way. "I got some new coloring books at your table, girls. Want to see?"

They nodded and followed him to the little table and chair set he'd put in his office especially for their visits.

After Cheyenne got them settled and they were happily cracking open a brand-new box of crayons, she turned his way. "Austin, what's going on?"

"Everything."

Hesitantly, she pulled over a stepping stool and perched on the edge of it. "That much, huh? Want to talk about it?"

They were kind of new to this brother/sister talking thing. Though she'd called often from California, he'd always felt that her worries over their father were misplaced.

In addition, he felt that she had never been willing to completely open up about everything that had gone down with her and her husband, Ryan. He wished that he could have been there for her. But because she hadn't reached out to him all that much, he realized that he hadn't completely earned her trust.

Once again he wished he knew the right words to get her to trust him. "There's kind of a lot to get into," he said. Deciding to sidestep things instead of delve into the truth, he said, "And maybe now's not the best time. The girls are here."

"The girls are always with me. And they're fine. Those crayons will keep them busy." Cheyenne crossed her arms over her chest. "So start talking. We've just come from visiting with Leah and Mrs. Hart, so I have all the time in the world."

The mention of Mrs. Sarah Hart only made Austin think of Dinah again. And yet again it made him get more than a little uncomfortable. "Before I talk, why don't you tell me what put that pretty smile on your face?"

"Oh, it's nothing all that special. I was just going to share that I got a big sale." A slow, sweet smile lit her face.

He could tell that she was trying real hard to act blasé, but there wasn't any reason to. She was pleased as punch, and as far as Austin was concerned, she had every reason to be. Ever since she'd come back to Roundup, she was doing her best to get her life back on track.

Because he was genuinely happy for her, a smile he didn't know he still possessed inside of him peeked out. "With whom?"

"The Ladies Auxiliary Club of Roundup."

He scratched his head. "I had no idea such a group existed."

"Me, neither." She shook her head. "But how it all happened is so amazing, Austin. I sold a necklace and earring set to Ace and Flynn Hart, and they gave the set to Mrs. Hart as a present. Then she wore it out to a meeting." Shrugging a little bashfully, she said, "I guess Mrs. Hart was showing them off, and next thing you know, they decided to give my bracelets as party favors for their next big benefit."

"That's real good."

"I think so, too! That's twenty bracelets right there."

"I'm proud of you, Chey."

Her smile faltered, as if she suddenly remembered his condition when she walked in. "Thanks. Listen, I don't know if you're up for it, but I thought maybe we could celebrate or something." Looking just as she did when she'd gotten her first 4-H ribbon when she was seven, she grinned. "We could go out to dinner and have a beer or a glass of wine or something."

Austin felt as if he was getting torn in half. He didn't have the heart to break hers by blowing her off.

But her entrance had given him the strength to be a little stronger than he thought he was. And now that he was back on track, a couple of those speeches from his AA meeting still rang in his ears like fire alarms. After finally getting up the courage to attend a meeting, he wasn't in a big hurry to become a failure there.

In addition, he was still focusing on that last bit of advice he'd gotten from Vanessa. That he didn't think about a lifetime of sobriety. Just a day.

"Um…listen. Going out sounds fun, but I kind of need to stick around here for a while." He stood up and enfolded her in a hug. As usual, his sister felt like a doll in his arms. She'd always been a petite little thing. He still couldn't bear to think of how she'd managed to carry that pair of babies inside her, and that was a fact.

When he pulled away, he said, "What do you say you go get us all a couple of burgers from the Number 1 Diner? We can eat them here."

"If I do that, will you tell me what's got you in a funk?"

He ached to confide in her. If anyone would understand

what he was going through and the problems he was facing, it was her. After all, she'd lived with Buddy Wright, too.

Shoot, she still was living with him. "I'll try."

Her gaze warmed. "I can work with that." After getting his lunch order, she left with a twenty out of the cash drawer.

After checking on the girls, he pulled out his phone and punched in the numbers.

"Austin?" Alan asked. "Is that you?"

"Yeah." His voice was husky. "Are you busy? I just need a few minutes."

"I've got time. What happened?"

He closed his eyes, pushed away his shame and made himself talk. "I almost closed up my store and spent the afternoon upstairs in the dark with a bottle of Maker's Mark." Austin ached to tell Alan more. About how it looked as if Dinah was never going to see him as anything other than a pretty handsome cowboy who was destined for failure. But he stopped himself. After all, he was only willing to admit one weakness at a time.

There was a pause at the other end. Austin felt the muscle in his cheek jump. No doubt the guy was about to tell him how many ways he wasn't ready to enter a program... especially one where he was expected to monitor himself.

"What stopped you from cracking open that bottle?"

"My sister. She came in with her girls and wanted my company." Still staring at the door and praying that it would stay closed for a few minutes longer, he said, "But if she hadn't..." His voice drifted off. Lord, his words sounded as stark and bleak as the back wall of his father's barn.

Maybe he really was as weak as Dinah thought he was. Otherwise, he'd be able to finish his sentence and utter the worst. With a silent curse, he forced himself to say it. "Alan, if Cheyenne hadn't come in here, I would have taken a shot of bourbon." Shoot, he probably would've taken a whole lot more than that.

"But she did. And you didn't."

He was taken off guard by the lack of disdain in his sponsor's voice. "Does that even count, though?" Forcing himself to admit everything, he said, "I have that bottle in my apartment. I haven't even had the courage to pour it out yet."

"Austin, it all counts. Staying sober isn't rocket science. This is all about admitting you have a problem and deciding to deal with it. Day by day." He paused. "Are you okay now?"

Surprised, he took stock of himself, looking for that familiar itch that made him want to jump out of his skin. "Yeah."

"Then whatever you're doing, do it some more."

"My sister went to go get burgers. We're going to hang out here for another hour or so."

"That'll do, right? So you're going to visit with your sister and not drink for a couple of hours. Good for you."

Austin was uncomfortable. Alan was making it sound as if he had something to celebrate instead of be upset about. "I wouldn't say any of this was good."

"Small victories, Austin. Remember, you've almost made it through another day."

That was it? He wasn't about to tell him he was ten kinds of loser? "That's all you've got to say?"

"Yep."

"But what about tomorrow?"

"Tomorrow, you can work on getting through tomorrow. And if you take that bottle back out but don't want to drink it, give me a call."

"Or Vanessa," he murmured, half to himself. "I've got another friend who said I could call…"

"That's right. Give her a call, too."

He hung up just as Cheyenne was walking down the sidewalk, a cardboard box with their lunches in her hands.

Though he felt kind of as though he was in the worst sort of daze, he strode to the front door and opened it for her. "This was the best idea I've had all day, Chey. I'm starved."

She beamed happily. "Me, too." Then to his surprise, she set down that box on the counter and flung her arms around his shoulders. "Oh, Austin. Things are really starting to look up. The girls are finally adjusting a little bit, I'm doing a job that I love, and you and me are getting back to how we used to be."

"I'm happy, too, sugar," he said, just to see Cheyenne's eyes light up again. The amazing thing was that he actually was.

Later, after they'd eaten their burgers, finished off a whole mess of fries, and the girls were once again happily coloring, Cheyenne said, "Want to talk about what's been bothering you?"

By now, the edge had worn off. If he brought it up again, Austin feared it would be like opening a wound, bringing back all the pain that he'd just pushed to the side. Plus, Cheyenne had enough problems; he had no desire to burden her with his garbage.

With all that in mind, he shook his head. "No, I'm good."

Her eyes—mirror images of his own—narrowed. "But you said you'd talk about it. And I was totally ready to listen."

She sounded as though she was missing out on a piece of candy. He chuckled. "Maybe another time, Cheyenne. I really am okay." For now.

"All right, then." With a weary sigh, she threw away her garbage and stretched her arms high. "Thanks for the break and for letting me celebrate with you."

"I was glad to do it." As a new idea came to him, he said, "You know, we can always build a jewelry case or something and showcase your stuff here. Instead of just selling a few pieces every now and then."

"You wouldn't mind?"

"Not at all. Matter of fact, I think it's a great idea. After all, you already work here when I'm on the road."

"You won't need to ask me that twice. As soon as I get a little bit more inventory, I'll bring some over."

The smile she gave him made him warm over. Almost as warm as a shot of that Maker's Mark made him.

But as she left, Austin had to admit that his sister's smile had given him something a liquor bottle never had—his self-respect.

Chapter Ten

It took twenty-four hours to obtain the search warrant. While Dinah made all the necessary phone calls, Duke once again contacted various secondhand retailers, other police departments and the innumerable online sites they'd been keeping tabs on.

But she was on her own today. Since Duke was only part-time, he was taking the day off, helping his wife, Angie, with their horse-biscuit business. If she didn't need him, he was even going to go help Angie man a booth at a rodeo this weekend.

All that meant Dinah had to be at the top of her game when she entered Wright's Western Wear. Of late, everything she and Austin seemed to say to each other was laced with double meanings. She was going to need to stay sharp if she didn't want to upset her investigation or make things worse between her and Austin.

But animosity brewed in the air the moment Austin looked up and watched her approach.

"So. You're back. At four o'clock, no less." His voice was flat, his expression full of disdain.

"I couldn't seem to stay away," she said sarcastically. Pulling out the folded sheet of paper from her pocket, which had been damn hard to get, she slapped it on the counter. "I've got the warrant."

To her surprise—and irritation—he unfolded it carefully and then proceeded to read every word. "This says you've got the right to inspect the property for saddles and tack." He smiled.

Caught off guard by the flash of white teeth, she said, "I didn't think you'd be grinning."

"I'm thankful that you're not about to start inspecting my underwear drawer. That's all. It would've been a big problem for me."

"I've seen men's underwear, Austin."

"Yeah, but I hardly ever wear any."

Before she could stop herself, she fell face-first into his trap. "What?"

"I go commando, Dinah. Unless I'm on the back of a horse, I'm practically free as a bird."

She was shocked. "Really?" And yes, that was her gaze sliding down to his hip area.

His smile widened. "Nothing comes between me and my Wranglers. So…want to check? Just to be sure you didn't miss a thing?"

Yes, she was flushing. "You just stand here while I do my job."

"Yes, ma'am."

Striding by him, she got a whiff of his cologne, and the scent seemed to linger in her subconscious as she walked directly to his storage room.

She was armed with pictures of the saddle and a silver-studded bridle that had been stolen from the Emersons. But the room was spotlessly clean and only held shelves lined with clothing, sporting equipment, and other odds and ends needed to run a store. There wasn't a saddle or a bridle to be seen.

Of course, she supposed he could have gotten rid of any incriminating evidence in the time it took her to get the search warrant.

Carefully, she walked through the shop, his office, even around the counter. She attempted to not disrupt anything more than she had to. But she also took care to be as thorough as possible.

But no matter where she looked, she couldn't find any sign of stolen tack. Not even the saddle she'd spied earlier. "Austin, where's that saddle with the roses?"

"I sold it."

"To whom?"

"Don't remember," he replied, his voice flat.

She couldn't deny the burst of regret that filled her. She didn't want him to be guilty—and she didn't really think he was—but her job was on the line. She needed to do everything she could to show that she was researching every angle—no matter how far-fetched. For him to be dodging her questions yet again wasn't good.

Feeling like half a fool, she held out her hand. "I need your house keys." She doubted he had taken to hiding bridles under his bed but stranger things had happened.

As she expected, Austin was taken aback. "My apartment is not the shop."

"But you live on the property, so technically, it counts." She'd made sure of that.

With a grimace, he handed them to her, but those striking blue eyes of his remained cloudy and cool.

Walking up the back stairs and carefully unlocking his door, Dinah didn't blame him. No one wanted their place to be searched for stolen merchandise.

Feeling silly, she looked under his bed and in his drawers for a silver bridle.

And in his living room for a saddle.

To her embarrassment she found herself opening up his bureau drawers, just to make sure no bridles were hidden inside. She tried to convince herself that she wasn't looking to see if he had any boxers or briefs neatly folded inside.

She found a scant three pairs. Neatly folded.

When Dinah returned to the store, she found Austin sitting in an old wooden rocking chair, thumbing through a magazine. As she looked at him, Dinah thought he looked something like a model himself. His blue plaid shirt curved around his muscles well, and the shirt, neatly pressed as always, emphasized his dark coloring and blue eyes.

When she stood in front of him, he got to his feet.

Schooling her features, she looked him in the eye. "I'm done."

"What's next?"

"I'll let you know. I'm sorry I had to intrude on your privacy like this."

"You're sorry?" Arms folded over his chest, he raised his brows. "And now…that's it? You're not going to handcuff me and take me in?" He lowered his voice to a gravelly drawl. "You're not going to lock me up, D?"

"Don't push me, Austin. I'm just trying to do my job." Inwardly, she winced. Even to her ears, she sounded stressed and whiney. Not the way a sheriff ever wanted to sound.

"Just your job, huh?" With a glare, he pointed at her cruiser parked prominently in front of the store. "Believe it or not, I'm trying to do mine, too. But I'm sure folks aren't too excited to come into a shop that the law has staked out."

"Don't exaggerate. I've hardly staked out the place, Austin."

"You couldn't have made it any plainer that you're here on an official visit." He shook his head. "What's with you, Dinah? I'm doing my best to work with you. Why couldn't you have simply walked over here from the sheriff's office like you usually do?"

His question made her realize that she probably had gone

a little out of her way to keep things professional. And she probably had desired to take his ego down a peg by parking her cruiser smack-dab in front.

Not that she didn't have the right to do that, though. "Austin, don't make this into something it isn't. The Emersons had a saddle stolen from them. Your truck was seen in the vicinity of their ranch last night."

"I can't change the way things are, Dinah." His eyes narrowed. "Used to be...neither could you."

His voice was raspy. For a split second, she was back in high school, partying too much and laughing with him too loudly.

Then she recalled going to another county to get a pregnancy test. And the total, complete band of fear that had threatened to choke her insides when she'd thought about telling her parents—and her brothers—that she'd gotten knocked up.

Brad, the boy she'd been fooling around with, had said the very same thing. That it wasn't possible to change the way things were.

At her silence, a muscle in his jaw jumped. "What? Don't you have something to say to that?"

"No." She hesitated, then leaned against the counter. "I know you're mad at me, and I don't blame you. But you have to try to see things from my side. Everyone and their brother wants me to have apprehended our thieves yesterday. I have to investigate every lead."

He blinked, as though trying to keep up with her scatterbrained mind. Then, as if he'd made a sudden decision, said, "Just so you know, I was at church on Monday night."

"Doing what? I didn't know there were services on Monday evenings."

"I wasn't at a church service."

"Do you mind telling me why you were there so we can

finish this up? Did anyone see you? Can anyone vouch for you?"

A bark of bitter laughter erupted from his lips. "Now I need people to vouch for me at church?"

"I'm trying my best to get your name cleared."

"Well, I'm trying my best to get you to realize that my name doesn't need to be cleared."

Austin Wright was going to give her an ulcer. She was sure of it. "Someone thinks they saw your truck near the Emersons' property, Austin. All I need is the name of one person who can vouch for you. Then I could mark you off my list of suspects, and then we wouldn't have to talk about this ever again."

"I didn't steal anything, Dinah."

"Then why won't you tell me who you were with?"

"Because I don't choose to."

"Why?"

"Because not everything I do is your business."

Her mouth went dry as pure disappointment warred with aggravation. "This isn't a joke, Austin. The robbery happened around ten o'clock. Please tell me who you were with at church."

"I can't, Dinah."

"Not even to clear your name?"

Pain crept into his gaze and seemed to settle there. Settling in like an old friend. "I'm sorry, but no."

The pressure of not doing anything was taking its toll. She had to at least look as if she had a suspect. Pete had seen his truck, and now the Johnson saddle was gone. So though it didn't feel right, she knew she had to do something. "I'm going to take you in."

He scowled. "You're going to take me in for questioning? Even though you didn't find anything here?" His voice was full of scorn. As if he was daring her to do something so foolish.

Feeling about a hundred years old, she nodded. "You have the right to remain silent," she began. "You have the right to an attorney…"

As she continued to Mirandize him, he raised his gaze and stared straight ahead, a twitching muscle in his jaw the only sign that she was breaking his heart.

Only the very slight tremor in her voice betrayed her feelings.

When she escorted him to her cruiser, Dinah realized that they both still had a whole lot in common. They both were remarkably good liars.

Chapter Eleven

She hadn't meant to keep Austin at the office long. But of course, the moment she'd gotten back to the office, the phone had been ringing. She placed Austin in the room set aside for questioning, along with a can of soda, and left him sitting in there, pissed off and irritable while she returned urgent messages.

Then, just as she was about to go question Austin some more, an emergency came up. There had been an accident involving a tractor trailer and two sedans on Highway 12, and they needed everyone within reach. She'd been forced to ask Duke to leave his family and go to the scene right away. Then she'd gotten another call. Things at the scene had gone from bad to worse. One of the drivers had died and another seemed high on something.

Though she was tempted to just let Austin go, she couldn't forget the fancy footwork she'd had to go through to get the search warrant. So, she asked Deputy Clyde Beck from neighboring Lavina to sit with Austin. After he arrived, she ran off to the accident scene. And spent the next six hours helping the officers on duty collect evidence, conduct interviews, talk with the coroner and provide medical care for a mother who'd sustained a few injuries because she wasn't wearing a seat belt. The lady just had happened to have a crying baby in a car seat, so more folks had been called to care for him.

Like so many things in law enforcement, what should have taken an hour or two had taken most of the night.

At almost three, after telling Duke thanks, she headed into Roundup and called Clyde on her cell. "Clyde, I'm so sorry. I'm on my way. I'll be there in twenty." Plus, she had to do something right with Austin. She'd never intended for him to stay there all night.

"Listen, why don't you just head on home? I've got this."

Though her body ached and her nerves were frayed, there was no way she could accept. "I can't let you do that, Clyde. I'll be there shortly."

"You can definitely let me sit here. Remember when you helped us a couple of months ago during the county fair? You worked like a dog for forty-eight hours straight."

"That was different."

"Listen, Austin and I got some food from the diner, we hung out, and now he's half-asleep on the cot in back. I'm perfectly happy napping on the couch. You get some rest and I'll see you in the morning."

"But—"

"Dinah, I'm telling you, there's nothing you could do now anyway."

"I can't leave him there all night."

"He's not getting tortured, Dinah. Go on home and get some sleep. I'll see you at six. That's in three hours, by the way. Sleep."

She did as he asked because he made a whole lot of sense. She was so tired and stressed it was a given that if she tried to do anything of value she would most likely make a bigger mess of things.

Pulling into her old Victorian, she barely made it to the bathroom to brush her teeth before collapsing into bed.

A hot shower and a pot of coffee almost made her feel human for her short drive to the office.

But when she arrived at five-thirty, things had gone from bad to worse.

Duke was waiting for her with a grim expression and Austin was sitting next to him looking madder than a yellow jacket stuck in a sprinkler head.

"What's going on?" She looked around. "Where's Clyde?"

"He just left. I got here early, deciding to start on some of the paperwork so you wouldn't have to do it all on your own...when we got a call." He sighed. "Dinah, there's been another robbery."

She checked her cell, then flinched as she saw that somehow she'd silenced the ringer. "Where?"

"My store." Austin glared.

"What?"

"Cheyenne just called over here. She went by there this morning. She got worried since I wasn't answering my cell phone." His expression darkened. "It's been locked up."

"What did Cheyenne say?"

"My store's been hit hard."

"Let's go." She was vaguely aware of Duke locking up the office as the three of them walked over to Austin's store.

Duke's dog, Zorro, kept pace with them, walking quietly by their sides through the early-morning fog. Absently, she ran her fingers through his thick coat.

Dinah was glad for the dog's calming influence, because she felt terrible.

Anger emanated from Austin with every step. She supposed she didn't blame him. She'd kept him from home for next to no reason, since she never had gotten a chance to talk to him further. It didn't even matter that she hadn't intended for him to be locked up.

Now chances were good that whoever hit up his shop knew he wasn't going to be there that evening.

When they walked in, she gasped. Beside her, Austin said

a few choice words loud enough to reverberate through the building. Their thieves had had a field day. Coats and other merchandise were on the ground, jeans were splayed all over counters. Leather belts and other accessories were scattered from one end of the store to the other.

Zorro lay down by the front door while Duke got out the digital camera and started taking snapshots.

After stopping briefly and staring at it all in wonder, Austin walked quickly to the back. There he called out, "Dinah?"

She had out a pen and paper. "What's up?"

"This." He pointed to the holes in the display. "Yesterday, two saddles were lying here." Turning to their right, he swore some more. "And at least five bridles and a rope. That's thousands of dollars of merchandise gone. I can't afford that. I'm toast."

Dinah felt so guilty, she almost would have rather he punched her in the arm. "I'm so sorry about this. I'm going to get these guys, Austin. I promise you that."

"Maybe you'd get somewhere if you started focusing on other people besides me."

He wasn't saying anything she wasn't already thinking to herself. Though Duke had stiffened behind her—obviously not appreciating Austin's critique—she felt that it was richly deserved. "You're right. I really am sorry. I know I messed things up. But when I never got a straight answer from you, I felt I had no choice. Look, I'll call Clyde again and see if he or the sheriff there can come out and help us some more. We'll fingerprint and take pictures. And I'll work nonstop until I get whoever did this."

Unable to face Austin's scorn a moment longer, she turned to Duke and mouthed a few choice swear words.

Duke closed his eyes. It was obvious he felt the same sense of frustration that she did.

"Austin, I hate to tell you this, but I'm afraid we're going to need to keep things like this for a while, so we can do our jobs."

"I know."

She turned around and gathered her courage to look at him directly again. And what she saw was a true surprise. All of a sudden, he wasn't yelling at her. Instead, there was the compassion shining once again in his eyes.

Austin had done a lot of thinking while hanging out in Dinah's sheriff's office. Around three in the morning, he'd come to the conclusion that if he hadn't been so intent on getting her riled up, she never would have brought him to her office.

His mouth had done a number on her, and he would have never attempted to rile up Duke or another sheriff that way.

He'd also known he should have been more up front with her. Pride was all well and good, but it had gotten in the way of common sense.

"Dinah, listen," he said slowly. "I'm upset with the situation, and I am mad. But I'll get over it."

"Really?"

He noticed the lines of stress and exhaustion around her eyes. He noticed the way she was holding herself together—as though she was in danger of falling apart by a good stiff wind.

He ran a hand through his dark hair. "I should have told you where I was on Monday night. I could have made your life a little easier." He leveled a hard stare her way. "Though you sure as heck didn't need to take me in, D."

"My apology was sincere, Austin. I know I overreacted."

His heart slowed a bit as he realized that was true. Dinah felt terrible about what had happened. And though he was pissed...well, he was pissed enough at the world. He wasn't real anxious to add her to his list.

Duke joined them. "So, what were you doing, Austin?"

Austin weighed his options. Part of him still ached to keep

his drinking problem a secret. But so far, that secret hadn't done him any favors. "Listen, I don't know how you're going to feel about this, but I was at a meeting at church."

"What kind of meeting?"

"It wasn't church related. It was—"

The door swung open and his dad strode in, looking upset enough to make a guy think his pants were on fire. "Dad? What the hell are you doing here?"

"Hoping to save your hide." Marching up to Dinah, he slammed a hand on Austin's front counter. "What the hell are you doing, girl? Arresting my son like he's some two-bit criminal? I bet you haven't even given him a moment to let him call a lawyer."

Dinah's eyes narrowed when Buddy slammed his hand on the counter again. "Mr. Wright, there's no need to hit things."

"No need to do what?" Buddy retorted. "Defend my family's honor? Just because I did a couple of things I'm not too proud of don't mean you can run ragged over my son."

Austin hated that his father even claimed him as kin. "Buddy, stop."

Dinah raised her eyebrows at his use of his father's name. But dammit, he didn't like to think of the broken-down drunk in front of him as anything but a distant relation. Here he was, rushing to Austin's defense, but he smelled to high heaven, though he didn't seem to be drunk.

Who even knew when he'd showered last?

Furthermore, his hair was scraggly, and his skin looked as sallow as ever. Most likely because he'd just come off a bender.

"Mr. Wright, you need to calm down," Duke said.

"I'm fine," Austin said.

She'd already apologized…and not a bit of it was his father's business.

Of course, his father didn't feel the same way. "Sheriff

Hart brought you over there in the cruiser. Everybody's talking about it." Looking around Austin's shop, with all the clothes and other merchandise in disarray, he added, "And now Cheyenne's told me that you got robbed."

Just a couple of moments ago, Austin was sure that this was the worst day of his life. But seeing his dad, thinking about everything he'd put them through?

In the grand scheme of things, Dinah taking him in didn't seem like all that big of a deal.

After all, his family had been through a whole lot worse. "Go on home, Buddy. Where is Cheyenne, anyway? I thought she was the one who found out the place was robbed."

"She had to go home to be with the girls."

"So who's taking you home?"

"I can still drive, boy."

Austin hadn't realized that his father still had his license. That was how distant their relationship had gotten. When Cheyenne had told him that she'd been driving their father around a lot, Austin had assumed that Buddy had done something to deserve his license being taken away. "If I need you, I'll let you know. But you need to go on out of here. You aren't helping."

Slowly, Buddy sagged, relaxing his militant stance, all of a sudden looking broken.

It pained Austin to see him this way, but not enough to feel sorry for him. It hadn't been easy growing up with a man who'd rather buy booze than food…and who would rather make money quickly than honestly. All his life, Austin had paid the price for his father's neglect, for his father's bad decisions. Even now, he didn't trust others, and he rarely trusted himself.

Making him feel like the worst example of a man.

After a few seconds of stunned silence, Buddy shuffled out.

Looking from him to Dinah, Duke cleared his throat. "I

think I've got enough pictures for now. I'm going to go get on the phone," he said before motioning for Zorro to follow him out the door.

When they were alone, the silence between him and Dinah turned palpable. And Austin realized he no longer had a thing to lose. His father was already his worst liability, and Dinah was already pretty darn sure that he was a carbon copy of the man.

It was either time to come completely clean or do what his dad had done unsuccessfully for most of his life: pretend to be better and smarter than he actually was. Put that way, there really wasn't much of a choice at all.

"Dinah, I was at an Alcoholics Anonymous meeting on Monday night," he said quietly. "I was there from seven until ten-thirty. I'd rather not tell you anyone's name to corroborate my story because I don't know anyone else's name. Just my sponsor, and it seems kind of a shame to give his name after he was kind enough to sit with me all that time."

Dinah's jaw dropped. "Austin, I…I had no idea."

He was so embarrassed, he made fun of himself. "You had no idea I was a drunk or that I finally decided to get help?"

Her gaze turned pained. "You're not a drunk. Austin, don't say such things."

"I'm not saying anything most folks haven't already thought, honey."

If she noticed that he'd slipped and called her an endearment, she didn't let on. "I had no idea you decided to join AA. How, uh, is it going?"

She'd asked the question quietly, and the expression in her eyes was kind. Almost as if she wasn't the sheriff and he wasn't the suspect accused of ruining the whole town. "I've only been to a grand total of one meeting." Because he was proud of himself—even though it wasn't much to be proud of—he said, "I haven't had a drop to drink in over a week, so I guess it's going okay. Well, at least on the right track."

"I'm proud of you."

"Yeah, right. I'm sure you're thinking that if I was a better man I could've nipped this in the bud all by myself." He looked away, and just so she wouldn't be the one to tell him the way things were, he added, "Shoot, for some reason, I'm the only guy around town who can't even handle one long-neck."

"For the record, I've never based a man's worth on whether or not he could suck down a few beers."

He was feeling so weak-kneed, he almost asked what she did take into account when considering a man's worth. But he caught himself in time. Instead, he forced himself to smile slightly and keep his pride. "Glad to hear it."

But of course, his snarky tone lay between them like a riled-up rattler.

Frowning, Dinah leaned forward, resting her elbows on the scarred countertop his dad had been pounding a couple of minutes ago. "Austin, is there any way we can just stop all this foolishness between us? I don't want to be your enemy. I really do care for you."

"How so?"

"I want to be your friend. I thought we once were."

He wanted to believe her. But his back was also stiff and sore from lying on a plastic mattress all night. "And this is how you treat your friends? Have them spend the night at your office?"

She sighed. "I know you don't believe me, but I really am just trying to do my job."

He felt like an ass all over again. Because the thing of it was, he admired a person who was willing to do what was hard. It was tempting to take things the easy way. Especially if going in that direction meant a person didn't have to make a lot of waves.

"I know you're only doing your job." He swallowed hard. "I'm sorry about Buddy showing up."

"You don't need to apologize for him."

"He should know better than to come barging in here, making a fuss."

Her eyes widened, then to his surprise, she totally looked as if she was trying her best not to laugh.

"Dinah? What did I say?"

"Nothing." She waved a hand. "I'm sorry. It's just that your dad's always been a piece of work." Her shoulders shook, giving evidence that she really was doing her best to hold it all in. "I mean, when hasn't he made a fuss?"

His surprise that she'd say such a thing flip-flopped to humor in the span of a few seconds. 'Cause the fact was, Dinah was right on the money. For all his life, his dad had seemed to thrive on creating waves where there was only a dry desert.

Buddy Wright's talent for adding drama to most any situation was almost a gift.

But never before had Austin been able to laugh about it. Next thing he knew, he, too, was grinning about his father's behavior.

"Remember when he got all riled up about the pony races?" he asked.

Her eyes sparkled. "When you were seven and he was sure everyone else in the area was a no-good, cheatin' liar?"

"Yep. I thought your brothers were going to have a conniption."

"They would've if my mom hadn't calmed them down." Smiling at him again, she sat up and cleared her throat. "Austin, if you could, please give me the name of your AA contact. I won't call. But I want something to document that there wasn't any way you could be a suspect."

Grabbing a pen, he wrote a name on a scrap piece of paper. "Here you go."

Without reading the name, she folded it neatly and slid it into her back pocket. "Thanks. I'll get out of your way now. My guess is that someone should be here to help with fingerprints within the hour."

"So you're going to be working all day?"

"Yeah."

"When are you going to make time to eat?"

"I don't know."

"Think you'd have time to get something to eat with me later?"

"You mean dinner?"

She looked nonplussed. He didn't blame her. Even he wasn't quite sure where the offer was coming from. But now that it was out there, shining like a beacon, he couldn't very well take it back.

"Yeah, I'm talking dinner."

"Not a date, though."

He didn't know what he wanted. All he did want was to be in her company for just a while longer. "Not a date. Just food. I mean, we both have to eat. And you did arrest me by mistake."

As he'd hoped, that got a rise out of her. "Austin, you don't need to keep reminding me every two minutes."

"So…what do you say?"

He thought she was actually going to consider it. For a moment, he'd even been sure that she was going to say yes.

But she bit her lip and shook her head. "I don't think it's a good idea."

He was disappointed, but he took it like a man. Shoot, only he would do something so stupid, anyway. Grabbing his old ball cap that was lying on a chair, he slapped it on his head, tipping it slightly as he backed away. "No biggee. I'll be seeing you, Sheriff Hart."

Dinah gave a little wave but didn't say a word.

Austin figured that was probably just as well.

Chapter Twelve

Driving down the highway, Austin instinctively kept looking for spots to make a U-turn. Though he knew there was no way around the fact that it was time he paid a visit to the old homestead.

His father's appearance at the store reminded Austin he had a sister and two nieces he was sorely neglecting. Besides doting on the girls when they stopped by or when Cheyenne worked for him at the shop, he'd done his best to keep his sister and her girls at a healthy distance. He loved them dearly, but he didn't want to see them all that much.

He didn't need a therapist to figure out the reason, either.

He ached to stay as far away from his father as possible. So much so that he'd been willing to sacrifice a relationship with a pair of four-year-old cuties in order to keep that divide deep and distant.

But, like so many other things in life, his head's good intentions didn't always jibe with what the rest of his body had in mind. The closer he got to the place he grew up, the more his palms started to sweat and the more his mouth went dry.

It was a familiar feeling, one he'd felt so often he could have bottled it up and sold it—if there'd ever been a need for true home*sickness*.

Usually when he started getting the sweats and the shakes, he figured it was also time to lessen his thirst and jitters with a couple of beers or a stiff drink. Or hell, both. With a te-quila chaser.

Now, of course, he was going to have to make do with re-membering his vow to himself.

But when he drove over the cattle guard and started down the short, narrow drive to the small home he used to call his own, Austin's hands began to shake even harder. Just like that, memories reappeared and warped in his brain, mak-ing him feel ill.

Making him feel weak and pretty much helpless.

"Get a grip on yourself," he said to the empty cab. "This ain't no way for a man to behave." When that bit of lame ad-vice didn't do much good, he pulled over onto the shoulder, took his hands off the wheel and breathed deeply.

Shoot. Cheyenne or his father was probably staring out the window, wondering who was parked on the side of the driveway in the dark.

More likely, he could be scaring the girls. Closing his eyes, he forced himself to think of something else. Some-thing that wouldn't rile his senses up like memories of his father always did.

A heartbeat passed. Two. Then out of the blue a familiar face flew into his mind. A pretty face with hazel eyes and a gorgeous head of brown curly hair.

Dinah, of course. Dinah, who could laugh louder than most people, whose eyes had sparkled with devilment back when they'd goofed off like teenagers do.

Dinah, lean and strong, racing her palomino Buttermilk in the ring. Pure determination lighting her eyes.

Dinah, chewing on his ass. Locking him up in her tiny interrogation room. Leaving him to rot there while she went off to save the world.

He knew he was slowly falling for her. Even though it made no sense. No sense at all.

"You can sure pick 'em, Wright," he scoffed as he pulled back onto the road and finished the short drive to the covered parking area.

Like he suspected, the moment he parked, Cheyenne came running out, Sammie and Sadie on her heels. Their hair was a shade redder than Cheyenne's auburn, but almost the exact match of his memories of her hair when she was small. His nieces peeked around their momma, looking as if they wanted to scamper out to greet him, but weren't sure if it was allowed.

He opened his door. "Hi, girls," he said. "Hey, Cheyenne. How are y'all doing?"

"Austin, I saw you pull off to the side." His sister assailed him the moment he slid out of the driver's side, his cell phone and a white plastic bag in his left hand. Concern etched her features as she looked him over. "What was wrong? Are you sick or something?"

"I'm good. I, uh, just got a text I wanted to read," he lied as he pressed a quick kiss to his sister's forehead.

His sister looked flummoxed, but she seemed to accept his excuse easily enough. "Oh."

As she looked ready to ask him more questions, he approached the twins and crouched down to pip-squeak eye level. "So...how're my girls?"

In typical shyness, they simply stared at him bashfully.

It seemed a little bit more charm was in order. "You two look pretty. So pretty I almost forgot that I brought y'all new crayon boxes."

Sammie's eyes widened as if he'd mentioned that he'd hung the moon. Reaching for her mother's hand, she used it as a lifeline to edge closer to her uncle. "Crayons?"

He held up the bag. "Uh-huh." Months ago, Cheyenne had told him that the girls were suckers for a perfect yellow-and-green box of fresh crayons. Kind of like how she used to be.

Though it grated on his sister, he brought the girls new

boxes and coloring books every chance he had. "Austin, you spoil them."

"Chey, everyone who's anyone knows new crayons work the best." Looking back at his nieces, he winked. "Right, girls?"

Little by little, small smiles lit their faces. Though she still stayed next to her mother, Sadie lifted her chin to meet his gaze. "Wanna come in and see my bear?"

"I thought you'd never ask," he said. "Wanna hold hands, just for a little bit?"

After a moment's hesitation, Sadie let go of her mother's hand and slipped her palm into his.

Austin's heart melted when he felt her small, pudgy hand nestled securely in his own. "Let's go see that bear."

After one step, Sammie reached for his other hand. "Hold mine, too?" she asked.

"Of course. I've got two hands and two best girls."

Sadie's eyes widened. "But what about Momma? Isn't she your best girl, too?"

After treating Cheyenne to a sly wink, he scowled. "No way. Your momma's my little sister. Yech!"

As he'd hoped, the girls smiled and started guiding him into the house.

The moment he stepped into the kitchen, the smell of old cigarettes and stale beer besieged him. He looked over his shoulder, half looking for his father.

"He's out at the barn," Cheyenne said.

"What's he doing out there at night? Is one of the mares sick?"

She shrugged. "I don't know. Every time I've tried to go out there to join him, he's practically bitten my head off. He says he's happier being out there than being in here."

"And you haven't snuck out there to see what's going on?"

he whispered as the twins kept pulling him down the hall, giggling to each other with every step.

"I haven't had a chance. He's hardly left the barn." She raised her voice. "And these two have been keeping me busy."

When they entered the girls' bedroom, which had one time been his, he couldn't believe the transformation. Gone were his old posters of rodeo stars and pinup girls. In their place was a plethora of pink and purple just about everywhere he looked. Pink-and-purple frilly curtains lined the windows. Drawings were neatly pinned on the bright walls. And about a hundred stuffed animals peeked out from every corner of the room.

"Sammie Sundell, do you mean to tell me you've got another bear? 'Cause it sure don't look like you need another bear."

"I did, Uncle Austin. I did."

"I got a horse," Sadie said importantly. "I told Momma that I was a real good girl."

"Sadie has been real good lately. Both of them have been good. Why, they sat nice and quiet the other day when I was working. A couple of ladies came over just to see me, and I sold four bracelets, two rings and a pendant."

"Momma was real happy," Sadie said.

"I'm happy with the news, too." Settling on the girls' floor, he straightened his legs and crossed them neatly at the ankles. "So who wants to play Trouble with me?"

Sammie's hand shot up. "I do."

Cheyenne, still standing in the doorway, cleared her throat. "Austin, are you sure you know how to play?"

"Cheyenne, if there's one thing I do know how to do it's play Trouble. Sadie, get out the game and let's go a few rounds."

"Austin, I'm so glad you came by. The girls are so happy to see you." Lowering her voice, she added, "Thank goodness."

He knew they still were having a heck of a time adjusting. So he kept his voice light and even. "I'm happy to see them, too."

"Can I get you something to drink?"

"A Coke would be real good, Cheyenne. And after you get me a drink, why don't you either play with us or go take a little break?"

"I've got a thousand things that need doing, but nothing sounds as fun as playing a game with y'all. I'll be right back."

They spent the next two hours good-naturedly playing games with the girls, sipping Cokes on ice and catching up on news.

Only after he'd helped Cheyenne get the girls tucked in bed and they were in the kitchen did his sister ask him anything personal. "So, how horrible was it when Dinah took you into the sheriff's office?"

"Not too horrible."

"I can't believe she kept you overnight."

"I don't think she intended that to happen. She was called away and I was stuck there."

"Still, she should have treated you better."

"It was no big deal. We simply had a miscommunication. Dad sure didn't need to talk to you about it." He hated the thought of Cheyenne sitting around worrying about him.

"Dad was concerned. And upset about your robbery."

"That did suck." He tried to grin, if only to ease his sister's worries.

"Still, though we're friends, next time I see Sheriff Dinah, I'm going to tell her what I think about her treating you that way."

Though his chivalry was kind of taking him by surprise, he rushed to defend Dinah again. "Cheyenne, it wasn't all her fault. Fact is, I wasn't being completely honest with her. If there was a problem, it was mine."

"How so?"

Austin wanted to shrug off her question, but he knew if the situation was reversed, he'd be peppering her with questions. And he wouldn't have waited so long to ask them, either.

It was on the tip of his tongue to tell her about his AA meetings. About how he was bound and determined to change and become a better man. But maybe it would be better for both of them if he didn't bring it up? Cheyenne had enough going on in her life without shouldering his burdens.

So, he took the safe route. Looking his sister in the eye, he said, "There's been some concern that maybe some of the stolen merchandise might be showing up at my store."

"Dinah thinks you stole it?"

He held up a hand to calm her down. "It's not all her fault. I do sell used equipment…"

"You're not a thief, Austin."

"I know I'm not. And I appreciate your support, too."

"Humph."

"Now, don't get into a lather. There's some other things that have gone on between me and Dinah that got in the way. That got in the middle of her direct questions and my evasive answers."

"Such as?"

"Such as things that aren't any of your business. Look, I'm going to shove off." Setting his empty Coke can and glass on the kitchen countertop, he said, "It was good to see you and the girls, Chey. I think they're doing better. You're doing a real good job with them."

Two lines furrowed her brow. "I don't know if they're doing better or not. They hardly ever leave my side. But we're working on it."

"That's all you can do."

"Austin, why don't you go out to the barn and see Dad, too? I know he'd appreciate it."

"No." He saw the flinch, and he felt bad for it. But not enough to apologize. He was done apologizing for his feelings for his father. Or his desire to remain distant from him.

To soften things, he pushed a wayward lock of hair away from his sister's forehead, smoothing the line that had formed between her brows as he did so. "I know you wish things were different, but can't we just accept it?"

"Not just yet. I want us to be a family."

"The family you're aching for just ain't going to happen, Cheyenne. You're stuck with the one you've got. We are what we are—all dysfunction and shot full of faults. If you want something different, you're going to have to go get your own."

"I already tried that. All I got was a husband who came back from the war so changed that he couldn't handle his life anymore." Quietly, she added, "I know he was hurting and dealing with a lot of stress from being in Iraq, but I can't forgive him for killing himself."

Inwardly, he flinched. Ryan had been a good man, a true hero. His suicide broke all their hearts.

Austin knew there was nothing he could say to make things better, so he kissed her brow. "Do you need some money?"

"No."

He reached into the back pocket of his jeans and pulled out his worn leather wallet. He didn't have a ton of extra money, but he could spare her three or four twenties. "Sure?"

"I'm okay. Put your wallet back, Austin."

"All right, then. But call me if you need something, okay?"

"I won't."

"Then I'll see you at the store. Bye, Sister," he said quickly. He fought a smile as he got into the cab of the truck. It had been a long time since he'd called her just "Sister," his childhood name for her.

As he drove back down the driveway, over the cattle guard

and back onto the highway, he thought about his family advice to Cheyenne.

And he thought about his dinner offer to Dinah. And how for a few seconds there, he'd been sure she was going to accept the invitation.

Now that he was almost off the hook in the suspect department, he decided he was just going to have to try a little harder in the dating department. Dinah Hart was on his mind—she wasn't about to go away—and he had a deep need to explore his feelings for her.

Chapter Thirteen

Dinah figured it didn't take a whole lot of gumption to step into Austin's store the next morning. All she really needed was a willingness to ignore her pride and let Austin walk all over her.

Judging by the way he had propped his elbows on the scarred counter as he watched her approach, he was prepared to do that. Whistling low, he looked at her with a definite sardonic gleam in his eye. "Here you are. Again. Dressed in a white blouse today, too. Where's your uniform, Sheriff?"

"Hi," she said, ignoring his dig.

And because she knew the drill, she stood there, waiting for him to continue.

He didn't disappoint there, either. "This must be the fourth time in as many days that you've called on me in the morning." His voice turned low and deep. "Best be careful. It's bound to be a habit."

Only because she figured she deserved his grief did she stand there and take it. Almost. "Are you done with your pretend flirting?"

"I rarely pretend to do that." Looking her up and down, he said, "So what gives? You anxious to see me so soon? Did you want to buy something?" Slapping his hand on the counter, his eyes went hard. "Or...let me guess. There's been another robbery. And I'm the prime suspect."

"Actually, there has been another robbery."

"Sorry, can't help you there. I was at my dad's last night."

Knowing just how much he didn't care for his father, she put off asking to see his back room. "Really? I have to say I'm surprised."

"I know. I don't go there much if I can help it. But Cheyenne and the girls are there and I like seeing them."

"Of course you do," she said gently. "They're sweet girls."

"Cheyenne's done a good job with them." He raised a brow. "So, if you're not here to interrogate me...what's the word?"

"The word is that I came to give you some pictures of some of the stolen saddles. I thought maybe you could be on the lookout for them, in case someone tries to sell them."

He took the photos without even the most cursory of glances. "All right. Thanks."

"And...I need to apologize to you."

"For what?"

She'd done so much damage to their relationship, she hardly knew where to begin. Sucking up her pride, she said what needed to be said. "For doubting you. For thinking the worst. For leaving you in the cell overnight."

As he folded his arms across his chest, she let her eyes follow the movement. Noticed how the muscles in his chest rippled under the thin cotton he was wearing.

She felt herself heat up again.

Oh, but it was time to get on out of there. "Well, that's all I wanted to say."

"Stop."

"What's wrong?"

He slowly walked around the counter, as if he—and she—had all the time in the world. "I don't accept apologies like that."

"You don't, huh?" Forcing her voice to remain detached, she said, "So what's it going to take?"

"I've had a lot of pain and suffering because of you, Dinah Hart. As far as I'm concerned, there's only one way you can make it up to me."

"And what is that?"

"You're going to have to go out with me."

She gulped. "Like, on a date?"

"Uh-huh. What do you think? Could you handle that?"

What she wanted to do was ask him how taking her out could make anything better. Or maybe she should remind him that they didn't have a lot in common.

But she'd never been weak. And she was tired of being everything to everyone and pretty much failing nonstop.

"I could handle it."

To her pleasure, he looked pleased. "Tonight?"

"I can do tonight. As long as nothing around here goes to hell."

"I'll pick you up at six-thirty."

"Where are we going?"

"Prime Rib and Fish House."

"That's kind of fancy, Austin."

"I'm that kind of guy, Dinah." He raised a brow. "Or have you already forgotten?"

He'd done it. He'd made her forget what they were talking about and what she was thinking. At the moment, she couldn't think of a single thing.

"I'll be ready."

"And don't you go and wait outside for me, neither. You wait on the other side of your door and wait for me to knock like a gentleman."

"How did you know I usually wait outside?"

"Could be that I can do a little bit of detective work, too, darling."

Flummoxed, she turned on her heel and left. Really wishing all of the sudden that there was another clothing store in Roundup besides Austin's store.

Because it would've been so nice to expend a little bit of her nervousness on some retail therapy.

HE GOT TO HER PLACE A FULL ten minutes early. Because he didn't trust her to wait inside for him, and no way did he want people to say he couldn't act like a gentleman if he wanted to.

As he headed up the walkway to the fussy Victorian, Austin took note of shades of cream and pink and beige on the curlicues that bordered the long porch lining the front of the house.

Thinking about Dinah living in such a place amused him. She was so businesslike and tough. She wore a hard armor to excel in her job, and Austin had to admit that her attitude worked. So far, he hadn't seen anyone give her lip. He didn't think it was just because of her office, either. No, there were always men who would risk flirting with a pretty girl, no matter what her occupation.

He grinned as he climbed the steps up to her second-story apartment, imagining the time she would give a man intent on showing her disrespect.

She opened the door before he had a chance to knock. "Austin, what are you smiling about?"

He walked in when it looked as if she was about to slip out before he even had a moment to pause on her front stoop. "I was just thinking about you," he murmured. Not really ready to start thinking about her as a sheriff again.

She looked a little worried. "What about me makes you smile?"

With any other woman, that would have been an invitation for a compliment. But with Dinah, she really did look worried. He would've given her a slew of practiced phrases, but two things caught him off guard.

The first was she was standing in front of him in a dress.

The second was that she was living in a room so creamy-white and soft he might have thought it was how heaven was decorated.

"This is pretty," he said, closing her front door behind him. "Where did you get all this stuff?"

Dinah looked down at her feet. "Oh, here and there. Garage sales."

He touched the bleached-white table, just big enough for two, before looking at the tiny kitchen featuring stainless-steel appliances. "This is a fairly fancy setup."

"It is. Just as poor Mrs. Jackson got these rooms fixed up, the bottom fell out of the real-estate market. She couldn't sell it, and I was able to rent a room here real cheap."

As if his feet had minds of their own, he peeked into her bedroom. The carpet was the only color in the expanse of white. Suddenly, he had a vision of lying with her on that bed. Her dark hair would look beautiful against the white sheets. And her compact, slim body?

He could only imagine how her skin would glow in the morning sun.

From behind him, she cleared her throat. "I guess all this girly stuff is kind of unexpected, huh?"

Feeling his way, he shook his head. "No. I think it's real nice, Dinah."

"Between the rodeos and the ranch and the sheriff's office…I get tired of being in a man's world."

"I could imagine that. There's nothing wrong with you being a girl, Dinah."

"Hey, now."

"Oh, I know. I'm supposed to call you 'woman' or 'sheriff,' or who knows what. But I like seeing you in a dress, and I like the idea of you going to sleep in a place that reminds me of a cloud bank."

Her mouth opened then shut. Kind of like a guppy.

He saved her. "Ready? For dinner?"

"Oh. Yeah."

"Let's go, then." After she locked her door, he held out his arm for her to take. And wonder of wonders, she took his elbow even though she didn't need to. He escorted her down the back steps and to her side of his truck.

For the first time in a long while, he felt he was worth something.

All because a woman like her was choosing to spend some of her precious free time going out with a man like him.

Chapter Fourteen

Austin didn't consume a single drop of alcohol at the restaurant. He didn't say a word about missing it, either. As a matter of fact, he didn't even look upset that she'd gone ahead and had a glass of wine.

To her surprise, he hadn't asked her to dance when a lot of the couples took to the floor in between their main course and dessert. He hadn't had dessert, either.

He hadn't asked about her job, hadn't asked about why she'd stopped barrel racing and hadn't pried into her family's business even once.

In short, going on a date with Austin wasn't much like anything she'd thought it would be. She'd imagined he would be a little loud, maybe a little full of funny stories about life on the rodeo circuit. She'd imagined that he'd lean a little too close and talk just a tiny bit suggestively.

Going out with Austin was starting to feel a lot like going out with one of her brothers—only there was less teasing. And Colt would have at least line danced.

But instead, Austin was kind of quiet. He seemed pleased to let her lead the conversation, even when all she was talking about was a ballistics class she'd taken a few years back in Bozeman. He looked happy to talk about horses and the latest movies. He didn't even seem to mind talking about their rodeo days or his latest events.

In fact, he seemed content to talk about everything and anything…and nothing at all.

All of that together made her feel calm, but a little on edge, too. She didn't know what to make of this contemplative and tame Austin. She was having a hard time equating the man she used to know—and the man she'd imagined he was—with the man she'd been keeping company with the past two hours.

Especially when he took her straight home at ten o'clock on the dot. Shoot, if she'd known he'd be so…staid, well, she sure wouldn't have worried about spending an evening alone with him. It seemed that Austin Wright could give a preacher a lesson in morality.

That was all good, right?

So why was she disappointed he wasn't a little more wild? That he hadn't held her hand or tried to kiss her?

This was a serious flaw on her part. Dinah knew she should be thanking her lucky stars that he'd been the perfect gentleman.

After he parked and turned off the ignition, he looked straight ahead, palming the key in between his clenched hands.

The sight of him attempting to be rigidly in control made her concerned. And because they were friends, she nudged his arm with her shoulder. "Austin? You okay?"

Her nudge seemed to shake him out of his reverie. He blinked, turned her way again. "What? Oh, yeah. I'm fine. Just fine."

"Are you sure about that?" He didn't look fine.

But instead of answering her directly, he unbuckled his seat belt and opened up his door. "This has been real nice, D. Let me walk you to the door."

There he went again, treating her the way no one else in the world seemed to. As though she was delicate. "I'm kind of the wrong person to worry about watching over, you know. I have no trouble walking alone in the dark."

His gaze darted in her direction. "I'm not walking you to the door to keep you safe, Dinah."

"Oh." Now she felt a little silly. Here he was being a gentleman, and she was straying farther and farther from ladylike behavior with every minute that passed.

Because she was still attempting to figure out how to act, she let him help her out of his truck. She leaned a little close to him when he curved his palm around her elbow and proceeded to carefully walk her up the steps. When she got her key out of her purse, she let him take it and unlock her door and turn on her light.

He smiled slightly and said, "Thank you for dinner, Dinah. I enjoyed myself so much. Good night."

That was it?

Gazing up at him, she stood motionless. Felt her body sway in his direction as she waited for his next move. Waited for him to kiss her cheek or hug her goodbye.

Okay, she was waiting for a whole lot more than that. She'd envisioned being wrapped up in his arms and held tight as he expertly kissed her good-night.

The way he had in her memories.

But when it became obvious that he wasn't going to do any of that, when it looked as though he was just fixing to turn and leave, Dinah knew it was time to say something. To do something. Because otherwise, they were going to be doing nothing. At all.

Taking a chance, she placed her palm smack in the middle of his chest. Right over his heart. "Austin, what is going on?"

His back stiffened. "What do you mean?"

"You've been so quiet this evening."

"Nothing wrong with that."

"No, there isn't." When he raised an eyebrow, she attempted to explain. "I mean there's nothing wrong with that at all. It's just...did I do something wrong?"

"Jeez, D. I can't seem to win with you. Either I'm partying or acting up too much. Or now...not doing enough."

"That's not what I meant, and you know it."

To her satisfaction, he glanced down at his hands, then looked her directly in the eye. "I know. Sorry."

"We've been friends a whole lot longer than enemies."

"We're not enemies."

"Then what's going on?"

He hung his head, looking suddenly as if he had the weight of the world on his shoulders. And shoot—maybe he did. "Truth?"

"Yeah."

"You're not going to like it..."

She was a sheriff, for heaven's sakes! Did he not think she'd seen just about everything there was to see? Plus, she had training. If he was having troubles, she was fully prepared to counsel him. To be the person in his life he needed. She wanted to be that person for him.

"Hit me with what you've got," she said, pulling him inside her apartment and closing the door behind them. "Talk to me, Austin. Tell me what you're really thinking. I can take it. I promise."

He still looked skeptical. But after a moment, he shrugged and got that determined look she'd seen often on the rodeo circuit: his game face. "All right. See, it's like this. All night..."

"Yes?"

He swallowed. "All night, it's taken everything I've had..."

She swayed closer. He reached out and held her shoulders. "Yes?"

"All night, it's taken every single solitary thing inside of me to not pull you close and kiss you."

She stood still, staring at him dumbly. "That's your deep, dark secret?"

"Well, yeah." In the dim light of her tiny, very feminine living room, his cheeks turned red.

Warning sirens started blaring in her ears. Not because of what he was saying…but because of how she was reacting to it. Because just like Pavlov's dog, she was reacting to his words, and she didn't seem to be having any control over it, either. "I had no idea," she said breathlessly. And damned if she didn't sound just like Roundup's answer to Marilyn Monroe!

"Well, now you do," he drawled. He took off his hat, tossed it onto the middle of her tiny kitchen table and jerked a hand through his hair, as if even his hair follicles were giving him fits. She knew the feeling—she felt as though her whole body was on fire. "I'm sorry, D. I didn't want to tell you how I was feeling."

The smart girl's answer would be a noncommittal shrug. Maybe an "it's no big deal."

But where he was concerned, she seemed to have lost all ability to form a smart girl's response.

She stepped close and asked the hundred-dollar question. "Why didn't you want me to know, Austin?"

"Why do you think?"

"I'm…I'm not sure."

His eyes narrowed. She gulped. Obviously he was beginning to realize that there was something going on with them that wasn't one-sided.

His hands shot out, wrapping around her waist and pulling her next to him. "Because I was afraid if I kissed you like I wanted to, if I kissed you like I used to…you'd get upset." His grip tightened, as if he was trying to hold on to the last ounce of his self-preservation. "Are you going to be upset with me, Dinah?"

All she seemed to be capable of was shaking her head.

Austin needed no more encouragement. Or was that discouragement? Leaning close, he pressed his lips against hers.

The contact was sweet. Tender.

It was kind of a letdown, really.

She opened her lips, let him know that things could progress to maybe something a little bit more. When he hesitated, she pressed closer to him, wrapping her arms around his neck, and reeled him in tight.

And then finally…he deepened that kiss, he slipped his hands along her rib cage, and soon he didn't need encouragement. Because he was kissing her the way she'd imagined him kissing her. The way he'd kissed her back in high school.

The way a grown woman imagines her Prince Charming would kiss her—once they were done with the G-rated fairy-tale ending, that is.

And, as Austin had obviously been afraid of, that one kiss became so much more, each kiss about ten times more passionate and out of control than the last.

She didn't want it to end.

Dinah was a smart woman, but she had no earthly idea how they ended up on her couch. And then her floor.

Or how Austin had managed to take off his boots without her noticing.

Or her dress. Or his jeans. Or her satin panties she wore only on special occasions. Which meant they were basically brand-new.

By the time they finally stopped for air, both of them were breathing hard. And they were naked, too.

Enjoying the feel of him on top of her—so heavy and warm and perfect—she shifted her hips, just to feel his smooth skin move against hers.

In answer, Austin braced himself up with one hand. Because his other was doing wonderful things to her breast.

"Oh, shoot. Look at us," he rasped. "Do you see what happened, Dinah?" he asked, his strained voice sounding as if he was lifting two-hundred-pound weights. "Do you finally see what I've been hoping to avoid?"

"I see that I'm stark naked underneath you."

"And that is why I shouldn't have kissed you."

"What do you want to do, Austin? Stop?"

Brushing strands of hair off her face, he jerked his head. "Hell, no." Leaning down, he whispered exactly what he wanted to do to her. "What do you think, Dinah? Can you handle that?"

Austin was proving that under that temporary church-boy exterior he was just as wild as she knew he'd be.

And because she rarely backed down from any challenge... she gave him the completely wrong answer.

"Of course," she murmured. And she smiled. Just before he did all the things he'd whispered about. And then he did them all over again, a whole lot more slowly.

Chapter Fifteen

Years ago, back when she was seven years old, Dinah had learned an important lesson: pretending ignorance wasn't always a bad thing.

It had all started when she'd sneaked her mother's special china teapot out of the china cabinet, filled it with water and then had her own little tea party in the privacy of her room. Things had gone well until one wrong move had slid that pot off the bedside table and onto the floor. Landing in five jagged pieces.

Dinah had stood there shocked. Heartbroken and scared, too. Her mother had *really* liked that teapot.

Quickly, she'd picked up those pieces and carried them into the kitchen, slicing her tender fingers in a couple of spots in the process. So much so that she'd left the whole mess on the kitchen counter.

When her mother had come in, she'd gotten in a tizzy about Dinah's cuts. She'd carefully tended Dinah, bandaged each finger, then gave Dinah a tall glass of chocolate milk.

Soon after, her momma had asked her, "Dinah, did you cut your hand on that broken teapot?"

There was only one answer. "Yes, ma'am."

"And how did it break? Do you know?"

That's when Dinah had an epiphany of sorts. Her mother

truly had no idea how the teapot had gotten from the top shelf of her china cabinet to lying in pieces on the kitchen counter.

Therefore, Dinah wasn't about to be punished. Unless she told the truth.

So she shrugged her shoulders.

Her mother narrowed her eyes. "Truly? You have no idea?"

"No, ma'am," she'd said in a rush. "When I came in here to get something to eat, I saw your teapot sitting on the counter all broken up." Figuring she might as well go whole hog, Dinah started the tears running. "Momma, I was just looking at the pieces and hurt my hand."

"I see."

"You know I can't reach the door to the china cabinet, Momma." Not without a chair under her. "Maybe one of the boys did it."

As she'd hoped, her mother took the bait.

Dinah had gotten cookies. Her brothers? A lecture.

Yep, sometimes it just didn't pay to fess up to the truth.

That had been a real good thing when it came to being caught following her brothers around in the barn, drinking beer when she was underage…or waking up in the shelter of Austin's very warm, very strong arms that morning.

Yep, sometimes a person shouldn't question how things came to be. Sometimes all she needed to do was simply accept what was what.

As a ray of sunlight shone through her bedroom window, landing square in her eyes as if she was fixin' to be interrogated, Dinah wondered how she was going to find a way to talk her way out of this one.

Because it was going to be difficult.

She'd lured Austin into her bed last night. If she hadn't pressed him, he would have walked away. If she hadn't kissed him with so much enthusiasm, he would have closed the door behind him instead of carrying her to bed.

No, he'd been the cautious gentleman last night, full of good intent. She? She'd played the part of the overeager, somewhat desperate hussy.

Thank you very much.

As she edged cautiously to the side of the bed, hoping she'd be able to somehow slide out and escape into the bathroom without him seeing, Austin's eyes popped open. They fixated on her like bright blue laser beams, practically daring her to go anywhere. She couldn't do it.

"Hi," she said. "I guess it's morning."

She could almost read his mind as he stared at her and began to review their past few hours together. For a split second, his eyes softened on her, taking in her bare shoulders as well as the rest of her that was trying like hell to keep covered by a thin white sheet. Then he smiled. "Whew. For a minute there, I thought I'd dreamed you up."

Oh, it certainly hadn't been a dream. "I did the same thing." Well, not really, but who was to know? "This kind of took me off guard. And we can't even blame it on alcohol."

"No, ma'am, we cannot." He smiled, looking extremely pleased about that. "Don't take this the wrong way, but I do believe this is the first time in a long while I've woken up with a woman when I've remembered every single second of the evening before."

Every second? That kind of made her nervous. "Hmm."

He continued talking, because, well, he was Austin. "Dinah, shoot, you were something else."

Something else? "I don't know how to reply to that."

"You don't need to, sugar."

That sounded like a good thing, but it was also kind of worrisome. "I remember everything, too. I suppose I need to remind you that I don't usually do things like that."

"What don't you do, Dinah?" he drawled. Teasing her terribly. "I mean usually?"

Oh! If she wasn't three shades of red and sitting under a sheet, she would have hit him. "Stop."

"Honey, don't be embarrassed. When I said 'whew,' I was simply remembering that trek from the floor to this bed. And the way you wrapped your legs around my waist and held on tight." He waggled his eyebrows. "It was impressive, Dinah."

It had been something, all right. She'd been clasped to him tighter than a cheap polyester suit.

She cleared her throat. "Listen, Duke has the day off, so I'd better get on my way. I've got to get in the shower and go to work."

"Okay."

"So…that means I'm going to need to get out of bed now." That, of course, was his cue to say adios. And maybe not look at her too closely in the morning light.

But instead of attempting to give her privacy, he folded his arms behind his head and smiled sleepily. "I hear you. You go do what you need to do. I'm just gonna lie here a minute."

Doing her best to pretend that she had nothing to be ashamed of, she walked to the bathroom. Trying to act as if she sauntered around naked all the time.

From the bed, Austin chuckled.

"Why are you laughing?" She turned to frown at him.

"No reason. I was just lying here admiring you. And thinking that for once I'm waking up happy."

"Oh." She hastily retreated to the bathroom and started working on her teeth.

After she'd gotten into the shower and closed the curtain, she heard Austin stroll in and say, "Dinah, after work, let's go over to Angie's."

She stuck her head out the opening and gave him a closer look. He had his jeans back on, but hanging low on his hips. "Why do you want to do that?"

"'Cause she's still got that litter of puppies, the ones that were dropped off at their barn door in the middle of the night. Isn't that something, the way people just turn things over to her?"

"It is a shame. How are they doing?"

"I didn't ask, but I imagine they're just fine. Angie has a way with animals. But listen, she told me about all them. They're brown and chubby, with floppy ears and stubby tails." His voice warmed. "Angie said they're as cute as all get-out."

"I was only kidding about getting a dog."

"I heard you had a good time with the puppies you took to the high school."

"Everyone loves puppies."

"Let's go see them. At the very least, it will make you happy."

"That's true." She turned off the water and hardly felt awkward at all when he handed a towel over the bar to her. "Thanks."

"How about I pick you up about seven?"

She wrapped the towel tight around her body, just over the curve of her breasts. "Seven tonight?"

"Well, yeah. Unless you want to spend the night together again."

So...were they a couple now? "Okay."

Next thing she knew, he'd pushed aside the shower curtain and had pressed his lips on her brow. "Thank you. I'm glad you're letting me do this."

She barely had time to respond before she heard her door open and shut, followed by the low growl of his truck reversing.

Too confused to figure out what in the world she was going to do, Dinah tossed off the towel, turned the water on hotter and stood directly under the showerhead, letting the hot bursts of water soak her shoulder blades.

What she should have done was thank him. Thank him for

reminding her that while she was a tough and capable sheriff, she was also still Dinah Hart. A girl.

SHE HAD A STEADY STREAM of emails and voice messages waiting for her when she got to the office. Luckily, no robberies, but enough other work to occupy her that she didn't take time for lunch.

In fact, she'd only just decided to go for a walk down to the Number 1 Diner to grab a cup of coffee and see if Sierra had any fresh pie, when her cell phone rang.

"Dinah, tell me that wasn't Austin Wright's truck in your parking lot last night."

"Ace, what the heck?"

"Just answer the question."

She'd played this game with him for most of her life. Ace loved to play big brother and seemed to think that part of the game meant he could be as bullheaded as he wanted to be.

She, on the other hand, had never cared for being either bullied or coddled. Adding a little extra sugar to her voice, she said, "Which parking lot are you referring to?"

"You know which one. Your parking lot. Your apartment's parking lot."

If Ace had his way, she'd still be having tea parties at home in her pink bedroom. "I see. So, is that what you're doing for fun now? Going out and doing surveillance in Roundup? Do I need to put you on the payroll?"

"Don't be a smart-ass."

She could almost see his teeth grinding. "If you don't want to talk to a smart-ass, don't call me up and start barking questions at me. I'm working." She bit her lip at the fib.

"I didn't know you and Austin were an item now."

Of course, it hadn't been something she'd really planned on, either. What had happened the night before had had a lot to do with an attraction that had been brewing between the two of them for practically a decade.

And though she'd enjoyed herself very much, she was mature enough to know that there was a big difference between enjoying a man's attentions for the night and wanting to eat breakfast, lunch and dinner with him for the rest of her life. "We're just feeling things out."

"Feeling things out?" he scoffed. "I bet. I hope you're on your way to go get checked for disease. That man's catted around more than most."

Standing outside the diner, she wrinkled her nose at Ace's words. And because she didn't like the inference that she wasn't smart enough to take care of herself, she inhaled and spat back a reply. "Ace, even though this is none of your business, I'll have you know—"

And just like that, she shut her mouth in midprotest. Because…oops. They hadn't used birth control. At all.

Standing there on the sidewalk, with half the town walking by and eyeing her curiously, she let her jaw drop.

Since when did she do things like that?

On the other side of the line, Ace's voice turned grumpier. "You'll have me know what, Dinah?"

She'd left him hanging, thinking the worst. And if she didn't finish up that thought real quick, he was going to march over here and get the full story.

But…shoot! What to tell him?

What if she told him the terribly awkward truth? That there hadn't been a prophylactic in sight? He was liable to beat up Austin ten ways to Tuesday. And then she was going to be manhandled all the way to the urgent care and be forced to get examined or something.

So she played it cool and resorted to that old lesson learned back when she was seven. Don't admit anything.

"Ace, I can't talk any longer. I'm just about to go get a piece of pie at the diner. But if you don't settle down, I'm going to tell Flynn on you."

"Wait a minute… What?"

"You heard me. Now leave me be. After I eat, I've got a ton of work to do. Roundup doesn't stay safe and orderly without me, you know. Bye." She clicked off. Feeling kind of proud of herself.

But a whole lot more foolish. Because Ace was definitely right. Austin Wright didn't have the best of reputations when it came to relationships.

She was still musing on that one as she went inside, nodded at Irene, one of Sierra's full-time waitresses, then sat in a back booth.

Irene walked over to her almost right away. "What can I get you, Sheriff Dinah?"

"Hi, Irene. How are you?"

"I'm hanging in there. My kids are driving me crazy at home, but that ain't nothing new." Pausing for breath, she smiled. "Hey, my Brandy said you and the puppies were a big hit at the high school. I think that was a real good way to chat with everyone. You going to go back anytime soon?"

"I'm going to try to. So, do y'all have any pie today? Please tell me that Sierra's been baking up a storm."

Irene warily glanced over to the counter near the cash register. There, Sierra and her aunt Jordan seemed to be having a heck of an argument. That was a surprise, given that Dinah had understood that they'd always gotten along pretty well.

After another moment passed, Irene said, "Sierra brought in apple and chocolate, I think."

Her eyes still on the two women, Dinah said, "I'll take a piece of either. And a large cup of coffee."

"Okay."

As Irene was about to turn away, Dinah lowered her voice. "Before you leave…what's going on?"

Irene bit her lip as if she really didn't want to say, then grudgingly reported, "Um, I'm not sure. Sierra's been real stressed out lately."

Dinah wanted to ask more, but Irene's expression told her that she wasn't going to get very far. It was obvious Irene didn't want to talk about her employer.

Well, she couldn't fault that. Leaning back in her booth, Dinah smiled. "Thanks for filling me in. Just the pie and coffee will be good for now."

"Okay, you got it."

While Dinah waited, her troubles surfaced all over again. Before she knew it, she was worrying about babies and venereal diseases. Ugh! The last two things in the world she wanted to be thinking about.

Instead, she subtly watched Sierra and Jordan. Of course, it wasn't all that hard to do, since their voices were getting louder.

Then, when Sierra was chatting with a newcomer, Dinah watched Jordan set a glass of water next to the cash register.

What happened next was like watching a train wreck. Sierra smiled at the customer, rang up another customer and knocked over the glass of water.

Jordan flinched when the water hit her in the middle of her chest. Their voices lowered, then raised, like waves crashing in the water.

Then Jordan mumbled something that sounded a whole lot like "eye doctor appointment."

Seconds passed. It seemed to Dinah that the whole restaurant went silent as everyone there waited for Sierra's response.

"Here, Sheriff," Irene blurted as she placed a generous slice of apple pie and a mug filled to the brim with coffee.

Dinah forced herself to look away from the two arguing women. "Thanks."

Warily, Irene glanced behind her before looking Dinah's way again. "You need anything else?"

Dinah shook her head as Jordan walked out of the restaurant, her Seeing Eye dog by her side…just as an obviously embarrassed Sierra turned around and rushed to the back.

And, Dinah thought with some remorse, Sierra was also a very good reminder that Dinah Hart wasn't the only person in Roundup, Montana, with problems.

She needed to remember that.

Chapter Sixteen

"Hey, Brother," Cheyenne said as she sauntered into the front door of Wright's Western Wear and Tack with a smile. "Look what I've got—two girls who are dying to see you."

Austin had been oiling a new King show saddle that had just come in, but dropped the rag and came over as soon as Sammie and Sadie appeared by their mother's side.

Slowly, he opened his arms for a hug. One by one, the girls hugged him. Austin counted their hugs as a huge milestone in his life. When they'd first arrived in Roundup, they'd hardly even look him in the eye; now their quick, gentle hugs reminded him that while a lot of things in his life were on the rails, his relationship with his nieces was improving.

He planted a noisy kiss on the top of each of their heads. While they giggled, he crouched down on one knee so he was eye level with them. "And how are my two favorite princesses?"

"Uncle Austin, we aren't princesses," Sadie said. "Don'tcha see what we're wearing?"

He tilted his head to one side. "What are you, then? 'Cause you look like princesses, dressed in your red skirts and sweaters. You two are the prettiest girls to have ever set foot in this store."

Sadie drew herself up to her full three-foot height. "We're

cheerleaders, Uncle Austin! Princesses don't wear *R*s on their sweaters like we've got."

"You sure?" With a wink at his sister, he said, "I don't know if I've ever seen cheerleaders who look like y'all. And no offense, but y'all seem a little short for the job."

"We're tall enough."

"We just got done with their first youth cheerleading class." Cheyenne rolled her eyes.

"Youth cheerleading, huh?" Little girl cheer programs sounded about as foreign to him as Malaysia.

Cheyenne shrugged. "I know, who would have thought? I did 4-H. But these girls don't want to have a thing to do with lambs or pigs. Instead, they just want to be decked out in sparkles. And they seem to do okay, as long as I stay in the room."

"Grandpa said we'd be real good," Sadie said.

"Oh, I know he did," Cheyenne agreed with a sassy smile. "That's exactly why I decided to give him a break and let him pay for these little classes."

At the mention of their dad, Austin's chest tightened and he tried to smile. "So what brings y'all by? Do you need something?"

"You," Cheyenne said with a wink. "I was wondering if we could convince you to come over tonight and have a cookout. Dad's making burgers."

With effort, he ignored the slight hint of longing in her voice. He knew his sister wanted them to be closer, and he felt the same way, too.

But they had a major difference of opinion when it came to their father. Cheyenne was willing to bank on Buddy Wright having changed for the better. He'd already gone down that road too many times to get sucked back into that fairy tale.

"I'm real sorry, Chey, but I'm afraid I've got other plans." Boy, he'd never been so glad to have those plans, too.

"I bet."

With the tension brewing between them, he knew he couldn't simply let things set and stew. Something had to be said. Warily, he snuck a glance at the girls.

Luckily, they'd lost interest in the adults' conversation and were looking at a pile of horse blankets in the corner. Seeing that they were safely occupied but well within view, he added, "Cheyenne, you know I don't want to be hanging out, grilling with Dad."

Staring hard at him, she said, "Are you ever going to forgive him?"

"For what?" He knew his voice was coming out harsher than he'd intended. But shoot, who could blame him? He had enough going on without dealing with his father's problems, too.

"For everything. Of course."

That was a tough question to answer. "I don't know."

"When will you? We're not getting any younger."

"I really do have other plans."

"Doing what?"

He didn't care for being interrogated in front of his nieces by his little sister in his store. "Not that it's any of your business, I've got plans with Dinah."

"Dinah Hart?"

"Is there another Dinah that you know of?"

"She thought you were a thief, Austin."

Put that way, he had the terrible feeling he was practically tripping over himself making more mistakes than his father ever did.

Especially when it came to women.

"Cheyenne, that's all over with now."

"Is it? 'Cause for a while there, it seemed that nobody in Roundup could talk of anything else. She ruined your reputation, Austin."

As if it wasn't already in the sewer? "Thanks for the update."

She visibly winced. "I'm sorry. I know I'm being harsh. But shoot, Austin. I find it interesting that you can act like what Dinah did was no big deal, but you still get all riled up about Dad."

The girls had gotten bored with the blanket and were within earshot. So he motioned them forward and redirected the conversation to the only thing he could think of that would have no return. "Guess what I'm doing tonight?"

"What?"

"I'm taking Sheriff Hart out to look at puppies."

As he'd expected, his nieces got all excited about the thought of the sheriff having a puppy. And of their uncle Austin getting it for her. And for the good chance that he'd bring the puppy by so they could cuddle him.

But his sister, unfortunately, was looking at him a whole different way. "You're buying her a dog?" she asked, pure shock and irritation singing in her voice. "Really? Don't you think things are moving a little fast between the two of you?"

A puppy wasn't a baby. And it wasn't toxic waste or a bomb or anything else her incredulous tone made it sound like.

He was just about to mention that to her, too, when a little bug buzzed in his ear. He knew that buzz. It was the one he got two seconds before they opened the shoot when he was on the back of a bronc.

It was the buzz he heard after he'd had two beers and was pulling out a third.

It was his body's handy internal warning system that signaled he'd just thrown himself into a dangerous situation.

Like an electrical switch had just been turned on, he remembered being in Dinah's arms. How soft and pretty she'd been. How passionate. How for a little while, he'd forgotten about all his problems and all the things that could have been or should have been.

Instead, he'd concentrated on her and loving her.

So far...none of that was bad. Was it?

Then, as if he'd been kicked in the ribs by an ornery horse, he gasped. With sudden clarity, he remembered they hadn't used birth control.

Which meant that he wasn't just a dumb drunk; he was an idiotic sober person, as well.

Cheyenne was looking at him strangely. "Austin? You okay?"

No. "I'm fine. Never better."

"You sure? 'Cause you're looking a little pasty."

He felt worse than that. Suddenly, his mouth was dry and his head was blank. And his conscience? It was burning as if he had a serious case of typhoid fever.

It was time to get these women out of his hair ASAP. "Correction, I'm taking her out to Angie's to look at the rescue pups," he said finally, walking toward the front of the store. "I don't believe any money will be changing hands."

"Are things that serious?"

He thought about being in bed with Dinah. Thought about the consequences that were maybe happening right that very minute. "They're pretty serious."

"I can't believe it."

"I know it's hard to get a handle on, but we're taking things slow." At least they had last night once they'd gotten to her bed. "Now, I hate to rush y'all, but I got about a thousand things to do. Enjoy those burgers."

As he'd anticipated, the girls accepted his brush-off easily, hugging his legs then scampering to the door.

But his sister merely stared. "Something's going on, and even though you don't need me meddling, I'm going to."

"I really don't need you meddling, Cheyenne."

"Too late. I'm going to call you later," she said.

Only Chey could make that promise sound like the world's worst threat. "Can't wait to hear from you," he muttered.

The moment they closed the door, Austin stared at his cell phone. The right thing to do would be to call up Dinah and mention that little stream of consciousness about birth control.

But she was a sheriff. Not some green girl.

So maybe she'd been on the Pill? Or had one of those IUDs or whatever they were called?

But it did seem kind of awkward to talk about that on the phone. Yeah, probably much better to discuss it in person.

All he was going to have to do was think of a good way to bring it up without reminding her that he was just about the biggest, most inconsiderate jerk in the state of Montana.

When he picked her up, it was pretty clear that this wasn't the right time, either. Dinah was edgy and uneasy sitting next to him.

"I almost called and canceled," she said the moment he pulled out of her parking lot.

"Why is that?" he asked, hoping he didn't sound as uneasy as he felt.

She didn't say anything for a minute, which was a surprise because Dinah Hart had never been especially shy when it came to putting people in their place. "I started thinking that maybe the two of us don't have much of a future together."

"Because?" He was glad he was driving so he didn't have to take his eyes off the road. If he got a good look of doubt and regret in her eyes, he knew he was going to start blurting things that needed a healthy dose of thought and care before they hit the air.

"Because when I'm with you, it feels like I'm going backward."

"Because of who I am? Because I'm one of those no-good Wrights?"

"No. Austin, no."

He peeked at her and realized with some shock that she looked frankly a little upset that he believed she thought the worst of him. "Then maybe you should explain yourself."

"Remember when we were in high school and we all ran a little wild?"

"I remember." He also remembered that his wild days had just been getting started while she, on the other hand, had had a few nights of being a little too crazy.

"I made some mistakes."

"Everyone does in high school, Dinah." He slowed to a turn and kept the speedometer low; they were now only minutes from Angie and Duke's place. But he sensed that she had something important to say that couldn't wait.

"No, I made a big mistake. I got carried away with the guy I was dating…"

"And?" He turned into Angie's property, happy to see Flynn's vehicle there waiting on them.

"And I thought I was pregnant."

If he'd ever been relieved to be parking the truck, it was at that moment. Given what had been going through his head ever since his sister had stopped by and he'd had his big realization, he didn't know if he could have kept driving without freaking out.

He brought the truck to a stop, exhaled and then stared at her.

"Funny you should bring that up."

"Funny why?"

"Funny, because I realized today that I neglected to keep you safe, Dinah."

His bald words lay there between them. Stark and naked.

Kind of like how he felt when he turned to her to see what she had to say about that.

Chapter Seventeen

Dinah had thought Austin could do nothing more to surprise her. But his statement, combined with the unflinching way he took complete responsibility for what had happened, left her speechless.

Now the figurative ball was in her court, and she had no idea what to say. Other than the truth.

"What happened between us wasn't only your fault, Austin. I was right there with you, and I forgot about birth control, too." Actually, it had been the very last thing on her mind.

He pressed his fingers on his forehead, as though she'd just given him a whale of a headache. "So…you weren't on the Pill? Or…anything else?"

"No." She felt idiotic. At the very least, she felt like the greenest coed alive. Here she was, supposed to be some kind of independent, capable woman…

And she couldn't even manage safe sex. Maybe she needed to get a couple of lessons from the high schoolers she was meeting with. They probably could be teaching her a thing or two about thinking ahead. She didn't even want to consider the possibility she might be pregnant. Then she thought of something else.

Even though it embarrassed the heck out of her, she had to ask. "Have you been checked out lately?"

Every muscle in his face seemed to turn to stone. "What?"

"You know. For any disease?" When he still stared, she sputtered. "Like herpes?" His blue eyes narrowed. "And since, you know, we didn't use any protection…"

"I don't have herpes. Do you?"

She winced. "No."

"Syphilis?"

"There's no need to get nasty, Austin."

Slowly, he took his hand off his door handle as the steam left him. "You're right. I'm sorry. Of course, we should have acted our ages. We should've thought about a whole lot of things. I'll go get tested."

"I will, too," she said. Though it would only be for what had just happened between them. She hadn't been in a physical relationship for years.

The muscle in his cheek jumped. "Fair enough."

Well, this was awkward. "Do you still want to go look at puppies?"

He blinked at her, and she realized that he'd assumed she didn't want to have another thing to do with him.

And while that might have been the smartest decision, it wasn't the truth.

"Yeah. Heck, why not?" He got out and stepped away, then turned and waited for her. "Come on, Dinah. Let's see if we can find you something cute to hold on to."

She walked to his side and tried not to notice how good it felt to stand next to him. His gait slowed to meet her own as they walked out toward one of Angie's barns.

"What's the story with this?"

"Well, it just so happens that Angie and I have become pretty good friends because of her horse treats and such. They're big sellers at the store. She's even filled in for me a time or two at the store when I've been on the road. Anyway, sometimes when she and Duke are on the road, or at a rodeo or trade show selling horse treats, I try to help out any way that I can."

"I thought Flynn and Ace were looking in on the animals."

"They do. Well, they're looking after the horses and other big livestock. But, you know, they're plenty busy."

Yes, they were, she realized with a sinking feeling. Flynn and Ace, and Colt and Leah, and Duke and the rest of her family had lots of things on their plates. She should have been reaching out to them a lot more than she had.

And she would've if she hadn't been so focused on her own problems.

Still chatting, Austin said, "Anyway, I told Angie I'd be more than happy to look after the dogs today. These puppies are too cute. Plus, they're not weaned yet, so the momma's got them pretty well in hand. However, I figured it suits everyone if I stop by here a couple of times a day."

She ached to compliment him on that. They all had busy jobs and sometimes offers only sounded good when they were offered, not when it came to actually doing the job for hours and hours.

But of course she couldn't say anything like that. There was no way she could get her words to sound anything other than condescending. Or avoid bringing into the open the fact that she hadn't even thought to offer Angie and Duke a helping hand.

She kept quiet until he opened the door, flicked on a switch and led the way into a cozy stall that had been converted into a home for the dogs.

The telltale sound of puppies whimpering and yipping claimed her heart like nothing else. Instantly, she forgot about everything but crouching in front of the mother dog and her litter.

"Oh, my gosh, Austin. There are puppies everywhere!"

"I thought so, too. There's eight of them. Aren't they as cute as all get-out?"

Cute hardly did them justice. Black and white and brown, with tiny pointy noses and pretty pink paws, the roly-poly pups were a funny combination of shepherd, terrier and who knew what else.

The momma dog looked at Austin and thumped her tail quietly. As though he had all the time in the world, he reached in and gently scratched her head. "How you doing, Bree? Those pups wearing you out yet?"

Bree answered with another tail thump, then a shift, moving her puppies around so she could get into a better position.

Like a child, Dinah flopped to the ground, sitting cross-legged, watching the puppies flop over each other.

And then Austin reached over and gently picked up a pup. Next thing Dinah knew, she was cuddling the puppy. "This is the best, Austin."

His gaze softened. "I thought you'd enjoy this. Puppies are the best thing I know of for guaranteed stress reduction. Bar none."

She yearned to thank him for thinking about her. For making sure she got just what she needed. But she settled for something a bit less personal. "I can't believe you remembered how much I liked dogs."

"It wasn't a difficult thing to remember, Dinah. You like dogs, and dogs like you."

His voice was low and sweet. Sinfully sexy, at least to her ears. And even though they were only talking about puppies, it felt like so much more. As he slid down to the ground beside her, laughing when a pair of pups rolled on the ground, a low, slow ebb of desire slid through her, making her think about being in bed with him again.

Making her think about being in his arms.

And it all made her rethink her goals and motivation, too.

Because it was now fairly obvious that there was a solid connection between the two of them, and it didn't have so much to do with old arguments and new problems.

Instead it had more to do with the warm comfort of a friendship that had grown and deepened through the years. Even in spite of themselves. She was just about to try and figure out how to talk to him about this when her cell phone chirped.

Of course the timing couldn't have been worse.

Holding it to her ear, she heard exactly what she didn't want to know. "I'll be right there," she said to the dispatcher.

Austin carefully pulled the sleepy puppy from her arms. "Let me guess…duty calls."

"Boy, howdy, does it ever," she said as she got to her feet and brushed the dust and hay from her jeans.

"What happened? Can you say?"

Wearily, she shrugged. "I can share it, sure. It's not a big surprise—there's been another robbery. Lord, but I'm so tired of this."

"Are you going to be okay? Do you want me to come with you?"

With any other man, she would have bitten his head off. No way did she want to be considered weak or as needing a man to look out for her. But instinctively, she knew Austin's concern was because he cared about her. It felt so genuine, she was tempted to accept his offer.

It would be nice to have someone to lean on for the next few hours. The community's nerves seemed to spike up another notch after every robbery, and there was no doubt in her mind that today's investigation wasn't going to be any easier. She didn't blame the townsfolk, either. People had a right to be able to sleep at night and not worry that some stranger was going to trespass on their property and take their stuff.

But she couldn't start relying on him. She needed to stay strong, to stay confident.

"Thanks for the offer, but I'll be okay. If you wouldn't mind, I need to get back to my car as soon as possible."

"Let's do it, then," he said, already leading the way out of the barn.

He drove her back to town as she stared into space and mentally prepared herself for the next few hours.

Not once did Austin act as if she wasn't doing something important. Never did he make her feel guilty for ruining their evening together.

When he dropped her off at her apartment, she already had her keys out and was prepared to do a quick dash upstairs, put on her tan uniform shirt, then hightail it to the Churchills' property.

"Thanks for taking me home, Austin."

"It was no problem."

Only when he pulled away did she realize that she should have spared a moment to thank him for showing her the puppies. And thank him for not minding that their plans had evaporated in an instant.

Maybe then they could have spared just one more moment and shared a sweet kiss.

Chapter Eighteen

Mr. and Mrs. Churchill were fired up and their ranch hands were, too. The moment she pulled up to the barn and parked, the older couple trotted out to greet her, their three ranch hands right behind them.

When she got out of her cruiser, they all started talking at once.

She held up her hands. "Whoa. You know I can't understand a thing y'all are saying, let along make any sense of it. Let me get my notebook and pencil out." Feeling vaguely like a nursery-school teacher, she gave the group of them a hard look. "While I'm doing that, one of you may decide who's going to speak first."

She bit her lip to keep from smiling as Mr. and Mrs. Churchill actually started arguing with the ranch hands about who was going to be the spokesperson. As she watched the lot of them, she noticed that two of the hands looked out of breath. Flushed. And Mr. Churchill's jeans had been sprayed with mud.

What in the world was going on?

Taking more time than needed, she slowly flipped back the pages on her notebook, carefully dated the top of the page, then finally looked up. "So, it's my understanding that y'all have had a robbery. Who's going to fill me in?"

Mr. Churchill inhaled. "This is my spread. I'll talk."

"Okay, then. What happened?" When he looked so excited he was about to burst, she said, "Sometimes it's easiest to start from the beginning."

"Okay." Mr. Churchill took a deep breath. "The thing is… we got 'em, Dinah."

"What? Ed, what are you talking about?"

"We identified the ranch robbers, Dinah!"

"Are you serious?"

"Serious as a heart attack! It's Rory Clark and his idiot friend Tracy Babcock!" Casey Landis, one of the hands, announced.

Dinah had known Casey almost as long as she'd known Austin. He, too, had been a part of their teenage wild bunch. Now he was foreman of the Diamond C, the Churchills' ranch. "How do you figure that?"

"Me and Garnet and Jimmy watched Rory's freakin' truck hightail it out of here."

Dinah looked at Garnet and Jimmy. "You sure about that?"

Garnet took off her hat and nodded. "I know Rory's truck, Sheriff Dinah. My dad's worked on it a number of times."

Dinah remembered that Garnet's dad owned a local auto shop. "Jimmy, what about you?" Jimmy was old enough to be her father, and she'd seen him plenty of times, helping with stock at rodeos.

"It was Rory and Tracy, Sheriff Dinah. Their Silverado raced through here like a bat out of hell."

"Damn near hit a herd of cows while they were at it, too. Broke two fence posts." Ed Churchill raised a brow. "Reckon they can be made to pay for that?"

"If it's them…yes." As in *hell, yes.* She was so ready for the culprits to pay for all the damages they'd incurred. "Now, sorry, but I need to know more information. What was stolen? What exactly did all of y'all see? I need the whole nine yards."

Mrs. Churchill wrapped her arms around her middle and

shivered. "Everyone, I say we can do this just as easily in the house around the kitchen table as out here under the carport." She waved a hand, leading the way. "Come on, y'all. Follow me. It's getting cold out."

Everyone seemed to be just fine with that idea, so Dinah followed the crew of them in. And then accepted a slice of peach pie and a cup of hot coffee, too.

While she ate and sipped, she gathered information. And before long, she was just about as happy as the rest of the group.

The Churchills had enough information in their stories to convince Dinah that they'd found the culprits. Quickly, she excused herself to call Judge Pruitt, explain the situation and ask for search warrants for both the Clark and Babcock homes. No way did she want anything to interfere with getting those boys locked up.

After Judge Pruitt promised he'd fax over the signed warrant to the office, Dinah continued on with her information gathering.

After writing the rest of the information down, as well as everyone's names and cell phones, she got ready to go inspect the barn. But there wasn't a whole lot of need. The Churchills had a photo of the saddle that was stolen. That was enough proof.

She slapped her hand on her thigh before getting up. "It all makes sense. Those kids have been a burr on my side for quite a while now."

"They're a handful," Ed Churchill agreed. "Of course, they always were. Their fathers never saw a lot of need in letting them be disappointed."

"Ever," Jan Churchill agreed. "You should have seen them in the school sports. Even back in middle school, if Rory wasn't picked to be quarterback, I swear, Farley thought the world was going to end."

"Before long, he'd be so in the coaches' faces, I reckon they thought their world had ended," Ed agreed. "Bad blood, there."

Casey nodded. "Spoiled rotten."

Dinah stood up. "I just wish I'd caught them a few robberies ago. Their shenanigans have brought a lot of people a lot of aggravation." She couldn't help but wonder what would have happened to her and Austin if she hadn't accused him of the robberies! "I'm so irritated, I could spit." Especially since Farley had been one of the men suggesting that a woman wasn't fit for the job and that maybe Duke would be a better sheriff!

Mr. Churchill patted her on the back. "Don't worry, Sheriff Dinah. We still believe in you. And now that we know who's been pulling this, I have to say that it's good you have eyewitnesses like us. If it was just conjecture, the Clarks and Babcocks would be gearing up to give you the runaround for sure."

"And you all feel up to getting the runaround?" It wasn't like they had a choice, but Dinah felt obligated to warn them. Accusing a doting father's son of a crime didn't always garner a person many favors.

Casey scoffed. "Heck, Dinah. I'd need someone a whole lot scarier than two uppity kids who are budding felons to take me down. I absolutely cannot wait to tell whoever whenever what we saw."

"Me, too, Sheriff," Garnet said. She smiled shyly. "A woman wouldn't last long around here without learning to stand up for herself."

Dinah was still chuckling about Garnet's quip when she pulled on her seat belt. To her way of thinking, she and Garnet were dealing with a lot of the same things. Both were in what was usually referred to as a man's job—at least in Montana. And, since Garnet hadn't been shy about voicing her opinion and the other members of the crew hadn't done a thing but look at her with respect, it looked as if she and Garnet were both managing to do okay in their chosen occupations, too.

As she was pulling out, her phone rang. "Please be Duke," she murmured to herself as she picked up. "Hello?"

"Dinah, what's going on?"

No voice ever sounded so good. "I'm so glad I'm talking to you." She might have been in charge, but she knew her job wouldn't be the same without Duke. He really was the steadying force in their partnership. In addition, he'd put in as many hours on this case as she had. He wanted the culprits caught as badly as she did.

"What happened? Are you okay?"

"I'm fine. Actually, I'm great," she said with a smile as she pressed her foot on the gas and let her cruiser fly. "Where are you at?"

"Sitting at home with Angie and Luke, watching *Star Wars*." His voice turned anxious. "Now tell me…what's up?"

"I was wondering if you were up for doing a little police work tonight." She knew she sounded giddy, punchy even.

"Tell me what the heck is going on. Now, cousin."

"Duke, we've got arrests to make!" Briefly she filled him in on the Churchills' stories and what they saw. "Isn't that something?"

"It's better than that. Shoot, if I had been there I probably would've ended up hugging Casey."

She grinned as she slowed the cruiser and approached the turn into town. "I almost did," she confided.

"Angie made the best dinner in the world. I didn't think anything could make me happier. But this has got to beat it."

Dinah laughed as she heard Angie good-naturedly tease him in the background. "Sounds like it's been a red-letter day for you all around."

"Yep. Though just about all of them are now."

The sentiment was so sugary-sweet, she knew she should want to gag. But instead, Dinah felt herself feeling more than a little jealous. It must be real nice to have that kind of relationship, where just having a home-cooked meal with the person you loved made the day complete.

Thinking about Austin, and about the closeness that was growing between them, she wondered if they were ever going to have that kind of relationship.

Or were they destined to always have so much baggage between them that they risked straining their necks just looking at each other over it?

She gripped her steering wheel hard. "Duke, can you meet me at the office in ten? Judge Pruitt is faxing over warrants that we need to pick up. I also want to call Deputy Beck and let his office know what we're doing. Just in case we need some backup."

"That's a good idea. Those boys are big, and I don't think they're going to take being arrested all that kindly."

She heard some rustling in the background and guessed Duke was already putting on his uniform shirt. "See you in fifteen."

It was less than an hour later when they got to the Clark residence. At first glance, it seemed quiet, too quiet for anyone to have been tearing through another ranch's land on an escapade. And she wondered suddenly if she'd been a fool to trust Casey and the rest of the Churchill crew the way she did.

Maybe she was on another wild-goose chase, and this time she'd decided to drag Duke and another sheriff's office into it. Just imagining getting this wrong made her stomach hurt.

"There's Rory's truck," Duke said, pointing to the tricked-out silver Silverado. "And dang if it doesn't look like it's recently driven through a muddy field."

There were mud splatters all over the truck. And to Dinah, so much mud had never looked so good.

"Duke, I think we've got him."

"I'm as pleased as you are, Dinah. And relieved. All I can say is that it's about damn time."

She parked the cruiser. "Ready?"

"Always."

Their arrival was definitely noticed because a trio of flood-lights illuminated the home when they pulled up.

When Dinah had called Deputy Beck he'd been almost as pleased as she'd been. "I'll come on out your way and alert another officer to stay near the phone here in case you need more backup. I can't wait to hear you've got those SOBs under lockdown. They've sure given us a run for the money."

Now Deputy Beck was getting out of his own truck and standing next to the Silverado.

Dinah was about to knock on the front door when it opened.

"What's going on, Dinah? Duke? Another robbery nearby?" Mr. Clark had just enough contempt in his voice to set Dinah's teeth on edge.

"As a matter of fact, yes. Where's Rory?"

Mrs. Clark came out and stood beside her husband. Dressed in a brown velour sweat suit and with next to no makeup on, she looked younger than usual. "He just got home a few minutes ago."

"We need to see him," Duke said.

"Can't it wait until tomorrow? He's getting ready to go to bed."

"It can't wait." Duke stepped forward. "Dinah, want me to go on in?"

"Hold on." Mr. Clark had his arms crossed over his chest and his somewhat insulting manner turned defensive. "There's no way I'm going to let you inside this house."

"I'm afraid that isn't your call," Dinah said as she motioned for Farley to step to the side.

Duke's phone buzzed as yet another vehicle pulled into the drive. "Clyde called us, Sheriff," the deputy said as he walked over to join them. "These boys have been such a pain in our backside, we thought we'd come out to give you some support."

"I'm obliged. If y'all wouldn't mind taking pictures of the truck, Duke and I will go get Rory."

In the living room she found Rory eating ice cream on the couch as though not a single thing in the world could ever bother him. When he saw Dinah and Duke, his spoon clattered to the bowl, but he kept up his cocky attitude. "What are y'all doing here?"

"Rory, stand up. I'm bringing you in for questioning."

"What? Why? What for?"

Duke smirked. "He's got all those questioning words down pat, D."

"Don't you know it." Turning to Rory, she repeated herself. "Come on, now."

His father appeared at the door. "Dinah, you can't manhandle my son like that. And there's no way in hell I'm going to let you take Rory anywhere. If you want to talk to him, you can talk to him here. Or better yet, you can ask his mother and me. He doesn't keep any secrets from us."

Over Rory's head, Dinah exchanged a look with Duke. "You sure about that, Mr. Clark?"

"I'm absolutely positive about that."

Duke chimed in. "Well, sir. If you are part of your son's thieving, we'll be needing to take you on in, too."

Paling, Farley Clark took two steps back. "You can't do that."

"Oh, yes, we can." Dinah smiled tightly. Really, she was

so darn tired of getting the runaround from these folks. "I'm the sheriff."

"Not for long. Not if I have anything to do about it."

To their surprise, Rory pulled out of her grip and actually looked as if he was contemplating making a run for it.

And that was the final straw. She spun on her heel, grabbed the young man's elbow, twisted it behind his back and pulled his ankle up with her foot.

Whether Rory was shocked—or she was still a fairly decent calf roper—Dinah wasn't sure. But whatever the case, in no time, she had him flat on the floor with his wrists and ankles pinned as if he was competing in a hog-tying event—as the hog.

After she read him his rights, Duke knelt down and clipped a pair of handcuffs behind the guy's back. Once the cuffs were clicked in place, Duke grinned her way. "Impressive, Sheriff."

She nodded her thanks. It really had felt good to be the one doing the takedown. She might not be as strong as her deputy, but she was certainly as scrappy!

Then Duke pulled Rory to his feet and started out the door.

Dinah couldn't help but take pride in the latest turn of events. She and Duke had been so frustrated for so long, it felt beyond good to prove her merit.

Mr. Clark didn't feel the same way, however. Pointing a finger at her chest, he said, "I'm going to make sure this costs you the election, Dinah. You made a serious breach in judgment coming over here and manhandling my boy."

Gosh, even though the writing was pretty much on the wall, Farley still didn't get it. "Mr. Clark, we have eyewitnesses who saw your son rob another ranch. He and his buddy Tracy Babcock, who is going to be arrested next, are our thieves. I'm going to pin your son with enough charges that he's going to wish he'd never begun this ridiculousness."

She eyed Farley, wondering if he'd been a part of it. But he looked so stunned and suddenly forlorn, she had a pretty good feeling that he didn't know a single thing about any of this.

"You'd best get a lawyer, Mr. Clark. I promise, you're going to need one."

When she got to the cruiser, she said to Duke, "I'm off to Tracy Babcock's house. Will you be okay?"

"I'll be just fine." Looking at Rory with more than a small amount of satisfaction, Duke added, "Matter of fact, I'm almost hoping that Rory here gets a little frisky. I'd love to take a turn at a little hog tying."

Dinah chuckled as she watched him leave and then went to make another arrest.

It was a very good night, indeed.

Chapter Nineteen

The stallion's body seemed to shake with suppressed anticipation as Austin carefully climbed on his back with the handlers' help.

After grabbing the rein with his right hand, Austin shifted slightly, tightening his thighs, mentally preparing himself as much as his body attuned itself to the animal.

"Feel okay, Wright?"

"Perfect," he replied to Custer, one of the handlers who seemed to have been around forever. "Feels just like old times," he said, his tone full of bravado in spite of the fact that he was about to go eight seconds—he hoped—on the back of a bucking bronc.

"And now, Austin Wright, on Black Magic, a horse with an attitude," the announcer declared with more than a bit of humor lacing his voice.

You got that right, Austin thought as the buzzer went off and the gate opened, and Black Magic burst out of the chute like a bat out of hell. Immediately, Austin shifted so he was marking out, taking care to keep his left hand up while his right held tight to the rigging.

And that was about the last coherent thing he thought before old Blackie did his thing.

He twisted, he spun, Austin felt himself be jerked forward

and back. Spun and bucked hard enough to feel as though he was riding a jackhammer one-handed.

His body sang in protest.

And he also had the terrible feeling that only four seconds had gone by.

Then old Black Magic did some sort of twist and bucking combination, snorted his pleasure and slammed his front hooves down hard on the arena floor.

The next thing he knew, Austin was flying off of that horse's back as if a spring had been loaded under his butt.

He landed with a smack on the ground, and the dirt under his body seemed to lift to meet him. A split second passed. He was half-aware of the clowns guiding old Black Magic away. Another wrangler helped him to his feet.

The crowd cheered as the announcer got back on the microphone with a whoop. "Old Black Magic proved once again that he's not fooling around! He got the best of Austin Wright in five seconds flat!"

Hobbling out of the arena, Austin shook his head. Bells were ringing in his ears.

"You okay, Austin?" Beau asked.

"Yeah. Sure," he said as he leaned against the fence and tried to not only find his breath but his bearings, too. "Damn, but I'm getting too old for this."

Beau laughed. "I've thought that a time or two."

Austin knew Beau was only being kind. Beau Adams lived for the adrenaline rush that came from time in the arena.

It used to be Austin had helped himself to a bit of that himself. But now he was only thinking that there was a whole lot better ways to make a buck.

"You want to meet us for a beer?"

Austin was tempted to keep things simple, but in the end, he decided to tell all. "I'm not drinking any longer."

"What?"

"It was getting a little out of control," he murmured. "I think I'm going to get cleaned up and head on back. I'm done." And he didn't want to be near any more temptation.

But to his surprise, Beau just slapped him on the back, his brown eyes shining with respect under the black felt rim of his hat. "Does this have anything to do with Dinah?"

"Not really. It was something I wanted to do for myself. Why?"

Beau looked at his boots, then met his gaze slowly. "It's just that the word is out that you've been spending time with my cousin."

Austin felt the muscles tense up in his shoulders. "And?"

"And I feel like I'm speaking for all of us Harts when I say don't screw around with Dinah."

"I don't intend to," he bit out.

Looking satisfied, Beau nodded. "Good. Hey, maybe one day soon we can go get a burger or something and catch up. You still eat meat?"

Giving him a sure sign with his finger, Austin laughed. "I'll call you soon, Adams. See ya."

Less than an hour later, he was sipping a Mountain Dew and pulling his truck onto the highway. He was sore and stiff, but a lot of the tension and anxiety that had been pent up in his body was gone. Now all he wanted to do was get close to Dinah and relax a bit.

Maybe that Black Magic had done his job in more ways than one.

He had now gone to three AA meetings, and he'd stayed sober, too. It had been the longest he'd gone without a drink since he was in his teens, Austin figured. His drinking hadn't gotten the best of him until lately, but back when he and Dinah and everyone else in their crew had been together a lot, it had been a common enough thing to hit it hard come Saturday night.

It was the weekend again, and because he didn't want to go home, and all his friends were at the bar, he'd decided to lie low and keep his hands and his mind busy.

But that had been the nature of his life, he supposed. He'd taken the difficult path instead of the easy one. Somewhere in there he figured it meant he had some gumption. But now he couldn't help thinking that maybe if he'd taken a little bit more care, he might be feeling ahead of the game instead of constantly ten steps behind.

Except for Dinah. Just thinking about how she'd felt in his arms made him smile. There was something to be said for a teenage crush.

His cell phone chimed just as he reached Roundup's city limits. "Austin Wright."

"Austin, it's me."

"Dinah, how's it going?"

"Great. We got them, Austin." Before he could ask her to explain, she started talking in a rush, each word practically tumbling over the next. "It all started with a call from the Churchills. You remember when we were at Angie's and I got called away?"

"I do." He couldn't keep the smile from his face. She sounded seriously cute. Almost giddy like a schoolgirl.

"When I got there, Mr. and Mrs. Churchill and Casey and Jimmy and Garnet all started talking at once."

"They were excited, too?"

"Yep. Listen to this, they'd all seen Rory's truck! The tricked-out silver Silverado! And they saw Rory and Tracy inside!"

He whistled low. Then kept his mouth shut as she continued, talking a mile a minute herself. "Rory tried to shake me off, but I got him to the floor in about ten seconds flat. It was awesome!"

He would have liked to have seen that. "I bet it was."

"And then Duke and I did the same thing with Tracy. Now all we got to do is figure out where they stashed all the gear. And Midnight, of course."

"Of course," he murmured as she started talking again, telling him about search warrants and photographs of saddles. Austin listened avidly. He was so proud of her, and her excitement was contagious. No matter how sore he was, she was making his problems seem minor.

Then, all too soon, she paused and added, "So that's what happened."

Braking at a stoplight, he said, "I couldn't be happier for you."

"You're…you're not mad at me right now, are you?"

"Why would I be?"

"Because, you know…I suspected you at one time."

She had, indeed. "Thanks to you, I got to spend the night in lockup." Now it didn't seem like that much of a problem, but he sure wasn't going to let her know.

"You know I'm sorry about that. Hey, I just realized you're probably still at the rodeo."

"Nah. I'm almost home. I got out in the first round."

"I'm real sorry about that, too."

"Heck, I'm not. If I was scoring points, I wouldn't be almost home. So…are you sorry enough to come apologize in person?"

"What?"

"Come spend the night with me, Dinah."

"You sure about that?"

"I don't think I've ever been more sure. Come on, D. I'll be home in ten minutes, tops."

"Well…"

He could tell she was carefully weighing the pros and cons of this. And there were a whole lot of cons and probably not too many pros. But that's what happened when a person over-thought things too much. "Just come on, Dinah. I'm the best offer you're going to receive tonight. I promise. Come over and I'll heat you up some soup and tell you how impressed I am that you solved your case."

"We just finally got lucky, that's all."

"Don't underestimate the value of luck, Dinah Hart. As a man who's spent most of his life looking to get lucky, I can promise you that it doesn't come around all that often."

"Getting lucky, hmm? Somehow I think that phrase has multiple meanings for you."

"Maybe. So, what do you say?"

She hesitated for all of three seconds. "I say I'll be there soon. Fifteen minutes or so. That will give you a moment or two to get organized."

Since he'd just parked his old truck, he smiled. "I'll be ready for you."

"And I'm walking over, so be on the lookout."

He still didn't care for her habit of walking alone in the dark. "How about I come get you? Then we can walk over here together?"

"Austin, if someone tries to accost me right now, I'm so keyed up, I'll probably be tempted to shoot them."

"Then in that case, I'll be sure not to sneak up on you."

"I'm fine."

"And I'm home. And by the way? I'm already out the door. Look for me."

He would've said that having Dinah in his arms was like old times, but there was nothing familiar with the feel of her. The way her hair fell over her bare shoulder caught his eye; the way her hazel eyes had widened then turned dark with passion while they were making love had been mesmerizing to him.

In short, everything about Dinah was special. She made everything in his past not matter anymore. He knew no other woman was ever going to hold a candle to her. He was falling in love with the woman who used to barrel race like lightning, who used to laugh so uproariously that the whole room would go quiet and who still possessed a sweet strand of doubt inside of her that she tried so hard to hide.

He loved that she was everything feminine in his arms, and everything tough and confident to the rest of the world.

Pulling away from him as dawn lightened the sky, she stared at him with regret. "I need to get up."

"I know you do."

Even though he'd completely agreed with her, she tried to explain herself some more. "Duke and I have a lot of paperwork to take care of. And a lot more questions to ask. I want that stolen merchandise back."

He rubbed her arm, gently letting his fingers slide down her silky smooth skin, enjoying the play of her muscles just underneath. "I hope you get the answers."

"And then there's the horse. Where do you think they stashed Midnight?"

He dropped his hand, preferring now to simply watch her mind click away. "No telling."

"I hope they didn't sell him someplace far away. That would just about kill my family. Colt, especially." She scooted a little farther, obviously intending to get up.

But then she looked his way with a bit of surprise in her eyes. "You're just letting me blather away."

"You don't blather, Sheriff. You weigh the pros and cons and make deductions admirably."

"Are you making fun of me?"

"Never."

"I really need to leave."

"I know."

"Except…"

"What?" he asked, right before she slid back down under

the covers and pressed herself against him. "Ah," he said. Wrapping his arms around her, he pulled her closer and pressed his lips to her neck. "Now, this I can help you with," he teased.

And then he proceeded to make love to her again.

Thirty minutes later, when she was running out the door, cell phone on her ear and cheeks slightly pink from his morning beard, Austin realized he could get used to this. He could get used to her. To a life with her.

Maybe he already had.

Chapter Twenty

The boys' lawyers were good. Dinah would give them that. But even the men with designer suits and expensive haircuts seemed to realize that the case against the boys was pretty strong.

However, no matter how hard they tried to bargain for leniency, they wouldn't budge on one thing: Midnight.

"We didn't touch that horse," Tracy Babcock said. Again. "I never even saw him."

"He went missing right after you two hit Thunder Ranch," Duke pointed out easily. "Right after you stole my uncle's saddle."

Dinah bit her lip. It was rare to see Duke so riled up about anything. Usually she was the one who went off half-cocked and he was the one calming her down. But Duke's impatience with the boys' high jinks mirrored her own. They might be small-town sheriffs, but they both were professionals, and they both had personal stakes in the events that had taken place.

"We didn't take the horse," Tracy said again, looking at his lawyer. "We didn't have any way of transporting him, anyway."

"Besides, that horse has a mind of its own," Rory Clark added. "It's not like we could have led him into a trailer without him causing ten kinds of a fuss."

Dinah had to reluctantly admit that Rory probably had a point. Midnight not only was a beautiful horse and a fine bucking performer, he was also as stubborn and willful as stallions came. No way would he have gone into a trailer willingly or easily for strangers.

In fact, it was far more likely that it would have taken at least an hour for Ace or Colt to coax him into a transport vehicle. There was no telling how long it would have taken these two knuckleheads.

The interview lasted another two hours. By the time they were done, she and Duke had a good start on where most of the stolen goods had been sold.

During this, she'd spoken to the district judge and set bail. It was high—but Dinah had a feeling that the boys' parents wouldn't think twice before posting the money and getting their sons home.

By the time the boys and the lawyers left, it was going on four o'clock, and both she and Duke were starving.

"I never thought I'd say this, but I've never been so tired just from sitting in a room."

"I agree one hundred percent." Rubbing her neck absently, she said, "I'd give my left hand for something to eat."

"Snickers stash empty?"

She chuckled. "Unfortunately, it's as dry as the Sahara." Plus, her stomach had been a little off lately. She was hoping that since the stress of the investigation was over she would get back to normal. But until then, Snickers bars weren't quite doing the job on her insides.

"How about I go get us some burgers from the Number 1?"

For a moment, she considered pushing aside the offer. But she needed to eat, and her usual salad option didn't sound appetizing at all. "You sure you don't mind?"

"Not in the slightest. Besides, I've got to take Zorro out anyway."

"Thanks." Looking at the list in front of her, Dinah knew she wasn't going to get to have a break for hours yet.

As she looked at the stack of messages, she debated who to call first. The mayor? Her mother and Ace? The Neimans?

She chose Austin. It didn't make sense at all. But perhaps that was okay. Right now, all she wanted was to smile for a minute.

"DINAH, HOW YOU DOING?" Austin said as he put down the stack of jeans he'd been sorting and held the receiver closer to his mouth.

"I'm so exhausted I think I could sleep for a week."

She did sound exhausted. He frowned, worried about her. "Why don't you come over tonight?"

"I better not."

"Sure?"

Amusement entered her voice. "When we're together, sleeping seems to be the last thing on our minds."

"It doesn't have to be that way." While it was true that he hadn't been shy about wanting to make love with her, he sure didn't want her to think that he had no manners. "I can look after you, too, Dinah. Shoot, I can even come to your place if you want. I can be there in a few minutes. I'll make you some tea or something and give you a back rub." Actually, he would enjoy pampering her a bit. He now knew that Dinah didn't let her guard down for many people. He liked knowing that he was one of the chosen few.

"That sounds great, but I better take a rain check. I'm still at the office."

He glanced at the wall clock. "It's getting near seven. You sure nothing can't wait until tomorrow?"

"I'm sure." He heard the shuffle of papers in the background. "Even if I wanted to take you up on a back rub, I don't have a choice. I've got enough paperwork to fill out and emails to return to keep me at this desk for hours."

"What about dinner?"

"Duke's bringing me something from the diner."

"Okay. Well, I've got my AA meeting tonight, but you can call me later." He couldn't believe it—he was finally starting to talk about his Alcoholics Anonymous meetings like they were part of his life, not a dirty secret.

She paused. "Have I told you how proud I am of you?"

That embarrassed him. "A better man wouldn't have had to go in the first place."

"That's where you're wrong. A good man deals with his faults and doesn't hide them." Her voice cracked slightly, making him wonder if she was just really tired—or there was more to her words.

"Call me later?"

"I'll try. Bye, Austin."

After they hung up, he worked for a while, then drove to the church for the meeting. When he walked in, he talked briefly with Alan and found himself chatting easily with a few of the other men there. He wouldn't call them friends, but they'd become important to him.

Then, just as he sat down and Alan stood up and began the meeting, he noticed a new face. It was a man old enough to be his father, and he was sitting there looking half resentful and half ashamed. Austin knew that feeling, of course.

And it also made him realize that it was time to move forward. If he was willing to deal with his drinking, and even have an open, honest relationship with Dinah, then it was time to deal with one other relationship in his life: his dad.

He was going to have to go pay him a visit. And this time, instead of only looking at the man's faults and dwelling on his painful disappointments, Austin realized he needed to look beyond them. It was time to try out this father-son thing once again.

Because everyone needed a second chance. He was living proof of that.

Chapter Twenty-One

Usually when Austin drove home he found himself taking every back road, just to make the trip out there last a little longer. Now, however, he was looking forward to chasing away the old ghosts and setting things right.

Sure, he wasn't perfect, and his family wasn't, either. Not by a long shot. But maybe they could learn to love each other in spite of their imperfections. He was slowly learning that love didn't have to mean you liked every little thing about the other person. Loving someone meant that you loved them no matter what.

When he pulled up and parked, a few windows were cracked and he could hear a television show on in the small living room.

Though he usually walked right in, this time he knocked softly. He needed to do what he came to do and didn't want to get sidetracked by Sammie and Sadie.

"Cheyenne, is Dad around?" Austin asked when his sister opened the door.

"He's out in the barn." Her grip on the door seemed to tighten before she schooled her features. "Is everything okay?"

"Everything's fine." For a moment, he was tempted to confide in her. To talk to her about everything that had gone wrong with him and their dad. But he didn't trust himself to deal with the pain twice in one night.

Plus, she had enough troubles. He didn't need to be a counselor to know that she, too, was hiding from memories of her marriage in the wake of Ryan's return from Iraq, his violent outbursts and even his death. The last thing in the world she needed was to be burdened with his problems.

"How are the girls?" he asked to buy himself a few more precious seconds before he faced his fears.

"They're good." She shrugged. "Sleeping, I hope." Still looking him over, she said, "I didn't know you were coming out tonight."

"I heard something at my meeting tonight that hit me hard. It made me realize that a visit here was long overdue."

She looked at him curiously. "Your meeting?"

"Yeah." Though his mouth felt like sandpaper, he forced himself to tell the truth to his sister. "I, uh, I've been going to Alcoholics Anonymous meetings, Chey. For a while now, I've known that I have a problem. I decided to get some help." He ached to say more, but he kind of hoped he didn't have to.

"So that's why you've been asking for Cokes."

"Yeah. I'm sorry. Until now, I wasn't ready to admit that I had to find some help." Especially not to his sister, who already seemed stronger than he was in so many ways.

"Are the meetings helping?"

"Yeah." He swallowed. "Actually, they are. They're helping a lot." Forcing himself to continue, he said, "I still want a beer about as badly as I want to breathe. But it's getting easier. That's something, I suppose."

He stepped back. He needed to have the conversation before he pushed it aside. That would be the absolutely wrong thing to do, even though it was tempting. "I'm going to go out to the barn."

"Okay. And…Austin?"

"Yeah?"

"Whatever you want to talk to Dad about? I think it's going to be okay. Heck, it might even go better than you think."

"Hope so."

Turning on his heel, he took the short walk out to the barn, memories stirring as he did so.

HIS DAD WAS DRESSED IN faded jeans, a black thermal long-sleeved shirt and an old brown barn jacket. He was sitting on an old metal chair in the middle of the barn when Austin entered. On his lap was a hardcover book, and over to his right was a reading lamp. An orange extension cord ran from the lamp to one of the wall plugs.

The sight took Austin by surprise. He paused, trying to come to terms with the sight in front of him—compared to the memories of his father.

"Hey, Dad."

"Austin! What are you doing here?" He put down the book and got to his feet. "Is anything wrong?"

Well, there was surprise number two. Growing up, he'd often come upon his father often just sitting by himself. But he'd been keeping company with a six-pack or a bottle of hooch.

Never sitting in silence reading a book.

"Nothing's wrong. Sit down, Dad. I, uh, thought it was time I came out to visit with you."

It was then that he noticed his father had reading glasses perched on the end of his nose. That was something new, too. "What are you reading? Anything good?"

He shrugged. "Just an old W.E.B. Griffin book. War stories." He glanced Austin's way. Almost shyly. "Ever read them?"

Austin had always liked to read, but hadn't taken the time to open in a book in years. "No."

"Oh." With care, he set his reading glasses in the middle of the book. "You better pull up a chair if you don't want me to stand up. I refuse to stare up at you like a child."

"Oh. Sure." He walked to the tack room and pulled out a step stool and set it across from his father, then sat down. And wondered how in the world he was going to be able to say what needed to be said.

Beside him, his dad kicked his legs straight out, well, his right one. His left never did bend correctly.

"Dad, whatever happened to your leg? Did you hurt it riding?"

"My leg?" His brows inched together, as if it pained him to think about it. "Oh, it's nothing. I hurt it in prison."

His father never talked about his time at the state prison. Matter of fact, Austin could only remember a handful of times in his life when his father had even mentioned the place. "I guess it was pretty bad there."

Buddy Wright looked at him with something akin to surprise. "Yeah. It was."

Austin winced. He hated to imagine what his father had gone through. He also hated that he'd never stopped to wonder what it had been like for his father.

As if he sought to calm him, his dad said, "Don't fret. My time in prison was bad, but it wasn't horrible all the time."

"Really?"

He smiled faintly. "Just most of it. Getting out of there was a happy day for me."

But of course, when he got out, Austin's mother had long gone. "So how did you hurt your leg?" Already Austin was imagining the worst.

"I'm not going to talk to you about that, Austin."

He was a grown man. He'd seen his fair share of ugliness. Given that, it had also been quite a while since anyone had attempted to shield him from the God's honest truth about anything. "The story is that bad?"

His father looked down at his heavily lined hands clenched on his lap. When he lifted his chin, he murmured, "There's some things a boy never needs to know about his father. This is one of them."

Austin tried that on for size…and realized his father was right. There were some things he hoped his own children would never find out about.

But there was one thing that needed to be shared. "Dad…a couple of weeks ago, I started going to Alcoholics Anonymous meetings."

His father looked completely stunned. "What brought that on?"

"The usual things," he said drily. "Drinking. Too much drinking."

"No. What really brought it on?"

"I woke up scared. I couldn't remember the night before. I started wondering what I'd done. And then realized that there were quite a few evenings that were a mystery to me."

"How are you doing?"

Austin shrugged. There, in the dim light of the barn, with the scent of hay and horse surrounding them, he knew that he could finally speak honestly. Not sugarcoat anything. Not pretend he was better than he was. "It's hard."

"Slipped yet?"

"Not yet."

"Maybe you won't. But if you do…"

"Yes?"

"If you do, you can always begin again."

That sounded like the voice of experience talking. "You're not drinking anymore?"

"No." His chin lifted. "I've been sober for almost a year now."

In spite of himself, Austin was impressed. "Who helped you?"

He chuckled softly. "You know who. You. And Cheyenne. And those girls. And the horses."

That made no sense. They'd always been there. Not that he was an expert or anything…but still…

His dad seemed to read his mind. "I know. It's about time, huh? I don't have a good excuse or a good reason. Just one day I decided that I was tired of spending all my time looking for the next buzz." He picked up his glasses. "So I took up reading."

"That's what got you through it?"

"Sometimes. Sometimes it was thinking about moments like this." He coughed. "I hoped one day we'd talk again."

Talk again. It didn't escape Austin's notice that his father wasn't asking for more than that.

A horse nickering in the back stall, his tone sounding deep and powerful, caught Austin's attention. "What you got back there, Dad?"

He swallowed. "A horse."

"Which one?"

His father got to his feet. "Well, there's a story about the horse back there."

"What is it?"

"That there is the Harts' horse."

Foreboding ripped through him as he attempted to prepare himself for the worst. "Which horse, Dad?"

"The Midnight Express."

Austin felt like whacking the palm of his hand against his head. Of course they would have the Harts' expensive stolen bucking horse. Because, well, who else in the area would besides those no-good Wrights?

Jeez.

Through gritted teeth, he said, "Tell me you did not go out and steal that horse."

"Austin, I definitely did not steal him." He walked slowly down the aisle, passed Cheyenne's pretty roan, passed Win Dixie, the stately quarter horse that Austin first learned to ride on.

Following, Austin stopped in front of the gelding and scratched the spot where Win had always liked to be rubbed. He did not want to get into a war of words with his father. But dammit, what possible explanation could there be for what the Harts' missing prize stallion was doing there? "Dad, tell me about Midnight."

"Not a whole lot to say," he said as he passed Prinny, the little mare Austin had picked up at a horse auction a couple of years ago, soon after he'd heard Cheyenne had had her twins. Prinny was skinny and skittish. Not really an abused horse, but definitely on the shy side. Austin had seen something in the silver horse that had melted his heart. And made him offer for her. He figured she'd be perfect for the girls' first riding lessons once she'd gotten used to being coddled a bit.

Right on the other side of Prinny's stall stood Midnight in all his glory.

Austin half expected the horse to be pushing against the fence or pacing in the stall. But instead of acting up, he was standing there relatively calmly as they approached.

No, he was standing there calm as could be. Austin had been on the backs of enough horses to know which ones had minds of their own—and this one surely did. For whatever reason, the beautiful coal-black stallion had found himself a temporary home in his father's barn. He seemed pretty pleased with it, too.

Now they just had to figure out what to do with him.

Midnight tossed his head at his father but didn't seem skittish around him. No, actually, he looked kind of as if he trusted him. His eyes were tracking Buddy's every move, and his ears were pricked a little forward.

As though he was expecting something.

Austin couldn't take the suspense any longer. "Dad, what happened?"

"One evening, I was sitting in here, trying to read and not drink. Talking to the horses, when I heard a commotion along the back fence. I went out there and, sure enough, there stood Midnight, looking worn-out and hurt."

"Hurt?" Austin slowly approached the stallion, but took care not to stand too close. It was very clear that the champion horse had little regard for him.

Buddy nodded, curving his hands over the top of the gate to the stall. "As best I can tell, old Midnight here had a bit of a run-in with a barbed-wire fence. His flank and side was cut up something awful." He frowned, staring at the horse. "And what's more, it looked like it had been that way for a day or two. So I took him home."

"Just like that?" He knew his voice was laced with sarcasm, but honestly, how could his dad be making it sound so easy?

"No, not just like that. This horse has an attitude like no other. But after I sat with him for a while, he calmed. Then I brought him a couple of carrots. He liked them fine. A little while later, he decided he didn't mind sharing a few of my apple slices, too."

"Sharing?"

His dad chose to ignore his snarky question. Chuckling softly, he said, "I talked to Midnight, too. Told him as ranches go, ours wasn't much. Not like the Harts' spread. But, if he was of a mind, I'd be happy to put him up for a while."

"You talked to the horse."

"Uh-huh. After a while, I guess what I had to say agreed with him, because he followed me to the barn and right into this stall." He glanced Prinny's way. "And I'd be lying if I didn't tell you that Prinny had a whole lot to do with his following me, too. Midnight is something of a ladies' man."

"Dad, why didn't you just call Ace Hart? Or Dinah?"

"To be honest, I didn't think about it at first. He was hurting and I was cold. Then he was hungry, so I let him munch on some hay." His eyes warmed from the memory. "Then I noticed him bleeding, so I decided to doctor up his legs and side."

"He didn't nip at you?"

"He wasn't real pleased, but he seemed to understand his choices. Then, when he seemed so content to be in the stall, I put it off until the next day."

"And then?"

"And then he settled in." He shrugged. "I don't have a good excuse, Austin. Every day I meant to give the Harts a call, but every day I also seemed to find a dozen excuses to wait. I was in no hurry to get arrested."

"You didn't think they'd believe you found him here?"

"Son, you haven't believed in me, not even when I told you I hadn't had a drink in almost a year. How was I going to expect a fine family like the Harts to believe I was better than they imagined?"

"I see your point." That had been his own fears working against him, Austin knew. He'd had too many memories of hoping his father would follow through on his promises—only to be let down all over again.

But as he gazed at his father and saw the hope and determination stirred up together in his faded blue eyes, Austin knew he was finally ready to lend his father his trust again. "But I'm willing to try again."

It was obvious his dad knew he was talking about more than calling the Harts. He blinked and swallowed. Turned away as if he was doing his best to gather his composure.

"Austin, are you sure? Because I have to tell you, I'm not real eager to get put in Dinah Hart's jail cell."

At that, Austin grinned. "Dad, for the record, I can honestly say that it ain't too bad in there. And the dinner they provided was pretty good. I've had worse."

His dad stilled, then looked at him slowly. "You're not kidding, are you?"

"I don't kid about jail cells, Dad. But...I've got a feeling that everything's going to be all right." He pulled out his cell phone. "Do you want to make the call or shall I?"

Chapter Twenty-Two

She should have known the whole family would go into an uproar. And boy, howdy, had they ever!

From the moment she called the house and spoke to her mom, Ace and Colt had gotten on the line. Then, next thing she knew, Duke had had Beau and Uncle Joshua adding their two cents.

And, typical for their clan, everyone had a very good idea about what to do with Midnight…and Buddy Wright.

All her life she'd let her older brothers manage the ranch business. Birth order didn't lie, no matter how tough of a sheriff she was. At home, she suddenly became Ace and Colt's little sister.

But this time she had to show her authority. So, while everyone was arguing and fixing to race out to the Wrights' ranch with a horse trailer, she raised her voice and fought hard to restore order. "Hold on, now. All of you."

Amazingly, all conversation halted. Next to her, Duke winked.

"What's wrong, Dinah?" Ace asked.

"These plans of yours. I am not about to let y'all go gallivanting down to the Wrights' right this minute."

"He has our horse," Colt said. As though there was nothing else that needed to be said.

Summoning her patience, she said, "Yes, Mr. Wright does.

But I spoke with him and Austin at length, and I don't think his reasons for holding on to Midnight are cause for us coming down hard on Buddy."

After exchanging a not-so-subtle look with her brothers, her mother stepped into the fray. "Dinah, I know you have a soft heart, especially toward Austin. But we've been worried sick about Midnight. We deserve to see him right now."

"Duke," she mumbled under her breath. "Want to help me out here?"

"I think it would be best if Ace and Colt came out to the ranch and met us there," Duke said soothingly. "Y'all can visit with Buddy and Midnight, then we'll plan on transporting him back to the ranch tomorrow."

"Why not tonight?"

"Because it's going on ten at night," Dinah said. "I know no one wants to get that horse settled in the middle of the night, and all our commotion isn't going to help Cheyenne's girls."

"What are you going to do about Buddy?"

"Duke and I are going to talk to him some more."

"And Austin?" Colt said. "What did Mom mean that you've got a soft spot for Austin Wright?"

Oh, brother! "That is none of your business."

"You're my little sister."

It was time to take control. "Colt, I stopped being a little sister a while ago. I mean, really. Now, Duke and I are heading to the Wrights'. If you and Ace want to meet us, I suppose you can. But no one's taking that horse anywhere tonight."

"Dinah—"

"Take it or leave it. If you want the offer, then I suggest y'all get a move on. Goodbye."

She clicked off with a resounding punch, then set her cell phone on her desk while she grabbed her uniform jacket. "Can you even believe our family?"

Duke clasped her on the shoulder as he went to grab his

own jacket. "Of course. If they acted any other way, I wouldn't recognize them."

As always, Dinah knew she'd chosen her deputy very wisely. Nobody could put things into perspective like Duke Adams.

"Let's roll," she murmured as they got into the cruiser. She just hoped and prayed nobody would put anyone into a headlock during the next few hours.

WHEN SHE GOT TO THE WRIGHT ranch, Dinah noticed Austin's expression before either of them said a word to each other. Suspicion and animosity showed bright in his eyes. And, she couldn't help but notice…a measure of protectiveness?

Just when it had seemed he was never going to forgive his father…he was currently standing in front of Buddy like a Doberman on patrol.

"You had to go get reinforcements?" he said sarcastically.

When grumbling from Ace and Colt erupted behind them, Duke did an about-face and sent her two brothers a meaningful look.

She paused, wondering if she was going to have to get in their faces, too. Midnight was their horse, but she was in charge at the moment. They needed to accept that her rules needed to guide them, not their own agendas.

When she heard no more complaining from the peanut gallery, she stepped forward and kept her voice easy and relaxed. "Not reinforcements. They are only here because they're interested in Midnight. They only want to see how he's feeling."

"Sure about that?"

"Positive." Deliberately moving around Austin, she looked at Mr. Wright, who was standing quietly. Not really cowed, but respectful. Actually, he was the best-behaved person there.

But what she noticed even more was his clear vision and

alert manner. This was a whole different Buddy Wright than she remembered. "Hey, Mr. Wright."

He nodded solemnly. "Sheriff."

"You've been calling me Dinah all my life. You don't need to stop now."

He straightened his shoulders. "I think it might be best if we keep things on the straight and narrow right now. I can't be letting no girl I call Dinah escort me to jail."

Beside her Duke chuckled. "Before we cuff you and haul you in, why don't we take a few steps back? How about you first tell us how Midnight came to be eating oats in your barn."

Buddy looked warily at his son. "I thought Austin told you everything."

"I did, Dad."

Duke continued. "Austin did talk to us. But I'd rather hear the whole story from you." Motioning to Ace and Colt, who looked as if they were staying in the background only by sheer will, he added, "And while we talk, would you mind if my cousins went and took a peek at Midnight?"

"I don't mind at all." He swallowed. "That's a real fine horse you got there, Ace."

Ace nodded. "Thank you, Buddy." Ace started forward, then stopped. "Dinah?"

She looked at Austin, who had visibly relaxed as if he started to realize that she wasn't about to start throwing her weight around. "Would you mind taking Colt and Ace on back? That way your dad and Duke and I can have some privacy."

"You okay with that, Dad?"

"It's a little late to start looking out for me, son," Buddy replied with a shadow of a smile. "Go on, now. Show those boys Midnight."

Austin didn't look happy, but he nodded. "Ace, Colt? The horse is back here."

After they walked in the barn, Buddy crossed his arms. "If I told you both that I didn't steal that horse, is there any chance y'all would listen?"

Duke laughed. "I've seen that horse in action, Mr. Wright. He's a fine animal. He's a heck of a bucking horse, too—a real champion. But he's definitely got a mind of his own. We've learned the hard way about trying to make Midnight do something he doesn't want."

Slowly, Buddy's lips curved into an appreciative smile. "I have a feeling you don't try the same thing twice. That horse is smart as a whip and twice as wily."

"You got that right," Duke said with a grin. Then his expression turned more serious. "Dinah, you ready?"

"Yep." Dinah felt a fresh batch of nervous anticipation. In a lot of ways, she felt as though her whole future was on the line. She didn't want to alienate Austin, or her family, or her reputation in the area. She was going to need to tread carefully and take careful notes.

But it was also time to begin. "So, when did you first see Midnight, Mr. Wright?"

"I'm not sure exactly, but it was near sunset, and I was just fixing to go sit in the barn and read—long story there—when I spied him limping along the back fence."

"Limping?"

Buddy rubbed his cheeks. "Maybe 'limping' ain't the best way to describe it. It was more like he wasn't wanting to do much. Kind of at a standstill. He was cut up something awful."

As he continued to tell his story, Dinah took copious notes. As she did, she began to get a real sense of Midnight's injuries…and how much Buddy Wright really had cared for the horse.

Her gut was telling her that he wasn't twisting the truth at all. It didn't stand to reason that he would, anyway. After all, what was he going to do with Midnight? Attempt to hide him from all of the Harts—and everyone else in Roundup who'd known he was missing—for the rest of the horse's life?

"Hey, Dinah?" Ace called out. "When y'all get a minute, come in here, would you?"

After another few minutes of questioning, she looked Duke's way. He nodded, letting her know without words that he was thinking the same thing she was—that there was no need to cart Buddy Wright anywhere.

When she closed her notebook, they all took a deep breath. "Well, let's go see what my brother wants, Mr. Wright."

When they walked into the dimly lit barn, Dinah's stomach seemed to grow even more knots. What did Ace want to show her?

And what was he going to expect her to do about it?

She didn't want to side with Buddy Wright in front of her brothers, but she didn't want to ignore Ace's concerns, either.

Feeling more than a little bit of trepidation, she led the way into the barn, Duke and Buddy Wright following her silently.

Chapter Twenty-Three

All of Austin's senses went on alert when Dinah, Duke and his dad entered the building. So far, neither Ace nor Colt had said anything derogatory about his father. But they could be waiting until they were all together to do that.

And the thing of it was, Austin knew he couldn't have really blamed the Harts. If the situation had been reversed, he'd be out for blood. On the other hand, Austin was feeling protective instincts he didn't even know he possessed rise up.

After far too long, he'd finally patched things up with his father. He didn't want the truce to last all of two hours.

When Dinah, Duke and his dad stopped in front of the stall, Midnight fussed a bit and twitched his tail. Almost as if he was showing off for company.

Then Ace waved a hand. "Look at this horse, Dinah."

She approached the stall, keeping a careful distance between her and Midnight. "What's up?"

"Look at his pastern. This horse must have been bleeding like a stuck pig."

"And?"

"And he's obviously been well treated and cared for." From his crouch, Ace looked up at Buddy Wright. "Mr. Wright, I don't know what issues Dinah might have with you. But as for me, I can assuredly tell you that we're grateful for your care of Midnight."

Colt nodded. "We're obliged."

Unexpectedly, Austin felt a lump grow in his throat at his father's stunned expression. His father had let so many people down in his life, Austin knew he never expected to be praised.

Especially not for his care of the missing prized stallion. Both he and his father had expected that he would be spending the night in a jail cell in Roundup.

"It was nothing," his father finally mumbled.

"Okay if we come by tomorrow morning to pick him up?"

They all turned to Dinah.

She shrugged. "Of course."

Colt nodded. "We'll see you in the morning, then. Night." And without another word, Ace and Colt left the barn together, their expressions easy and relaxed, as if they weren't doing anything more than going home after an eventful evening.

His dad faced Duke and Dinah. "What happens now?"

Duke glanced Dinah's way before replying. "We're going to need to talk to Sarah and see if she wants to press any charges."

Just when Austin opened his mouth to refute that, Duke raised a cautioning hand. "Everything needs to happen in its own time, Austin. Don't fly off the handle."

"Sorry. You're right."

"Mr. Wright, we'll stop by here tomorrow morning, too. Look for us around ten. Okay?"

"I'll be here."

"Good. Then we'll see y'all in the morning. Night."

When they started walking away, Austin strode to Dinah's side. "Can I speak with you for a sec?"

"Now's not the right time. I can't give you any more information."

He lowered his voice. "I wanted to talk about us. Not the horse. Not anything else."

A new warmth flickered in her eyes. "Why don't you call me later? I should be home in about an hour. We could talk then."

"I'll do that." He reached out and squeezed her hand gently before releasing it and letting her get on her way.

When they were alone again, he turned to his dad, who was staring at Midnight. His father looked weary. "Dad, you okay?"

"Yeah. Considering that I thought they were going to cuff me and cart me off, I'm doing just fine." He shifted on his feet. "I think this horse pretty much saved my life."

"How so?"

"He trusted me. It's been a long time since I'd felt that." His hands curved around the top railing of Midnight's stall. "I'm not saying that I haven't deserved everything that I've gotten, but there's something about this horse that made me see myself just a little bit differently than I have in a very long time."

Guilt washed over Austin before he firmly reminded himself that his own feelings hadn't been without good reasons. He'd been burned time and again by his father's failings.

But Austin was stronger now. Wiser, maybe. And he knew that the opportunity to feel worthy was a gift that couldn't be ignored. "In that case, I do believe I'm going to be indebted to a horse."

His father laughed. "Me, too."

"I'm going to head on home now."

"Anxious to see your girl?"

"Dinah?"

"Of course. It's fairly obvious that there's only one woman you have eyes for."

Now it was Austin's turn to smile broadly. "I am anxious to see her, but I won't be seeing her tonight. She's kind of tied up. I am going to call her, though."

"A good woman is worth more than gold, Austin. That's one cliché that's absolutely true."

"I'll remember that." He paused, then stepped forward and held out his hand. "Night, Dad."

His father's large, work-roughened hand squeezed his own. It wasn't a hug, but it was a first step. "Night, Austin."

"You heading back to the house?"

Taking a seat on that fold-out chair again, his dad shook his head. "No. I'm good here."

When Austin turned and took that lonely walk back to his own truck, he realized all of a sudden that he wasn't all that lonely after all. He had a woman who was expecting him to call…and a father he felt he could finally have a relationship with again. Life had never felt so sweet.

"CRAZY HOW THINGS WORK OUT, don't you think?" Duke asked as they left the Wrights' ranch and headed back into town. "All this time, we've had both the thefts and Midnight's disappearance on our minds. Now both cases are solved."

"It is amazing. Especially since I can't claim that our superior detective skills had much to do with solving either mystery."

Beside her, Duke puffed up a bit. "Speak for yourself," he said. "You might not feel like we earned this success, but I sure as hell do. I've spent hours on the computer and on the phone attempting to track down the whereabouts of expensive saddles."

"And expensive horses." Feeling buoyant about it all, she said, "I can't thank you enough for all your help, Duke."

"I was only doing my job, same as you. And before you get all mushy, let me just tell you that I think we make a real fine team, just the way we are. For the record, I have no designs on being Roundup's sheriff."

"So you've heard about those rumors, too?"

"Of old men thinking a young woman can't manage things well? I have. But they're wrong, Dinah. You're doing a great job."

"Thanks. Hearing you say that? It means the world to me."

After a moment, she said, "Duke, tell me the truth. Do you think Ace and Colt really are going to let things slide with Buddy Wright, since they've got Midnight back?"

"I can't speak for them, but my best guess is that they're going to be fine with not pressing charges. It's not in their nature to be vindictive. Plus, anyone who knows Midnight knows that that's a horse who knows his own mind. I feel that way. I know Beau does, too."

"I hope you're right," she said when she parked in front of their office. Now that things were getting better between her and Austin, she sure didn't want anything to disrupt the fragile bond.

"You're going home now, right?" Duke asked when they got out of the cruiser.

"I'm going. I'll be back over here early, though."

"Great. I'll meet you here."

"Hold on. You're not on the schedule tomorrow. Why don't you let me call you if I need another set of hands?"

"Sure?"

"Positive."

Then, grabbing her purse, she took the short walk back to her Victorian, knowing as she walked that there was a definite spring in her step.

Because boy, howdy, they'd found that horse!

Chapter Twenty-Four

The knocking on her door the next morning at 8:00 a.m. matched the pounding in her head. She'd woken up to the worst case of nausea in the world.

Third time that week.

Her cheeks still damp from the warm washcloth she'd just run over her face, she opened the door to the tantalizing sight of Austin holding two steaming cups of coffee.

Unfortunately, the coffee smelled anything but tantalizing. "Ugh!" she gasped, making an abrupt U-turn as she practically sprinted back to the bathroom.

To her mortification, Austin was on her heels. "Dinah? What's wrong? You sick?"

"Just a minute," she mumbled before heaving into the toilet once again. Thank goodness she'd closed the bathroom door.

But he opened it up and walked right in. "Dinah, honey?"

"I'm okay. Maybe." She sat on the white tile and blew her nose. And…wished he would leave and forget all about the sight of her vomiting.

But instead of being grossed out, he sat next to her on the tile floor. "What's going on?"

"I don't know. I'm just really queasy all of a sudden." Daring to take a peek at him, she glanced his way. The concern in his eyes made her own eyes water.

What the heck? What in the world was going on with her?

Against her will, she started tearing up. Covering her face with her hands, she mumbled, "I'm really sorry you had to see me this way. Why don't you go on and I'll give you a call later?" Like in a couple of years when she wasn't so embarrassed!

He didn't budge. "Maybe it's the flu. Are you achy?"

She thought about it. "No."

He reached out and planted a palm on her forehead. Just as if she was one of his nieces. "Hmm. I don't think you have a fever."

"I know I don't."

"Maybe it's food related. Did you eat something bad last night?"

"I didn't eat at all," she said with a slight whine in her voice. Hating that whine, hating her tears, she sat up straighter and tried to get her act together. "I just woke up this morning feeling pukey," she said while swiping at her cheeks. "I'm sure it's nothing."

"It might be something."

"Doubt it. I mean, if I'm not sick, what could it be?"

His eyes widened. "You could be pregnant."

"I couldn't be." But now that she thought about it…the idea took hold and wrapped itself around her head. Gaping at him, she stared. Then when her tears started flowing again, she leaned back with her head against the tile wall.

He turned so he faced her. "Dinah, there's nothing wrong with you, is there? I mean, you can get pregnant. Right?"

"I guess I could."

"Is this the only time you've gotten sick in the morning?"

"No…" With a gulp, she added, "It's happened a couple of times lately."

"So you could have morning sickness."

He sounded so matter-of-fact. So pleased. As if he was a detective who had solved a difficult case.

It was a little discomfiting.

What she ached to do was give him what for. To remind him that she was a grown woman. And a sheriff.

She didn't lose control. Except with Austin.

She didn't do things on the spur of the moment. Except with Austin.

And most of all…she wasn't the type to not learn from her mistakes. She'd already had a pregnancy scare once. When she was little more than a child. Seventeen!

No way was she going to go through that again. And especially not with Austin Wright.

Slowly, he got to his feet, then bent down and held out a hand to her. "Let's get you off the floor, sugar."

Sugar? "Austin, I feel better now. I think I'll take a shower."

"All right," he said agreeably. "But first, will you do something for me?"

"What?"

"Go back to bed."

With effort, she kept her expression neutral. "I'm not sick, Austin. And I'm not going to go sit in bed. I've got things to do."

"I know."

"Good. Because I've got about a thousand pounds of paperwork—"

He spoke right over her, as if his was the only voice of reason in the room. "If you don't want to lie down, how about you go sit on the couch instead? It won't take me but a few minutes until I get back."

Get back? "Where are you going?"

"To the pharmacy, of course."

This time she gave in to temptation and rolled her eyes. "I am not sick, Austin."

"I'm getting a pregnancy test, Dinah," he said over his shoulder. "Now, try to relax. Put your feet up."

She was still attempting to process his words as he walked out her door and got ready to embarrass her in front of the whole town of Roundup. No doubt, his pregnancy testing would be remarked upon.

As would his truck outside her front door.

Next thing she knew, she'd be getting phone calls from concerned townspeople about her "condition."

All of that made perfect sense.

What didn't was why she settled on the cushions, leaned her head back against the armrest, closed her eyes and waited for him to return.

AUSTIN TIPPED HIS WHITE FELT Stetson at Ms. Perry, sitting next to the register near the RiteWay's entrance. "Ma'am."

"Hello, Austin. What brings you in today?"

"Just needed a few things. I won't be but a minute," he added as he pretended to be cool as a cucumber while walking down the feminine-protection aisle.

Immediately he was assaulted by pink-and-white plastic packaging. But surely this was where those little kits were?

He stood in the middle of the aisle and stared as all the boxes appeared to blend together.

Ms. Perry seemed to be keeping a careful eye on him. "Austin, you need something special over there?"

"No, ma'am." He stepped toward the left. Near the condoms. Okay. Surely he was headed in the right direction? Then, like a floodlight had focused on his face, he found what he was looking for.

On impulse, he grabbed three kits. Just in case the first two didn't read right.

There was no way in hell he wanted to walk down that aisle again anytime soon.

He'd just turned on his heel and had started the long walk of shame toward Ms. Perry when the store's door opened and

Colt Hart rolled in. The moment Colt caught sight of him, his easy smile widened.

"Hey, Austin," he said.

"Hey. Colt." Why was his face flushing?

"Ace, Gracie and I got Midnight back to the ranch this morning, no problem."

"That's good. Real good. How's he doing?"

Colt grinned. "He's just as cocky as ever. He sauntered out of that horse trailer and into his corral like he owned the place and was finally returning home."

In spite of the trio of pink boxes in his hands, Austin grinned. "That's great. Really great. I'll, uh, see you later."

"Sure." Colt's gaze drifted to his hands, noticed what Austin was holding and froze. "So. Where are you off to now?"

"Work," he lied. Austin directed an even stare Colt's way. Practically daring the guy to question him.

Colt raised his brows and for a moment looked as if he was going to say something stupid. Then he got smart and simply nodded. "Oh. Sure."

"See you later."

"Hey…Austin?"

"Yeah?"

Colt stepped close enough so his voice wouldn't carry to even Ms. Perry's eagle ears. "Just in case there isn't a big demand for pregnancy tests among your customers…if you knocked up my sister, you'd best be prepared to answer to the lot of us."

"Thanks for the warning."

Of course, what Colt didn't realize was that Austin didn't need any threats or warnings. He cared about Dinah, and he was willing to do whatever it took to make her happy.

Because then he would be happy, too.

But there was no way he was going to start opening his heart to Dinah's brother. "Like I said…see you later." Then he stepped up to Ms. Perry, plopped his purchases on the counter and practically dared her to comment on them.

After a momentary pause, Ms. Perry scanned all three boxes and placed them neatly in a white paper sack. "Eighteen dollars, Austin."

"Here's a twenty."

"That'll do." The moment she gave him his change, Austin hightailed it out of there.

Dinah was asleep on the couch when he returned. Once again he enjoyed the sense that she only let her guard down with him.

He stood over her for a moment, liking how sweet she looked. Dressed in leggings and an oversize flannel shirt, the collar and cuffs frayed from frequent washings, Austin figured she could easily have been mistaken for one of the high school girls she'd been talking to recently. With her eyes closed and her hair far curlier than she usually allowed it to be, Dinah seemed smaller. Far more fragile.

Funny how he'd become accustomed to her alert, perceptive gaze settling on him.

As if she'd suddenly felt his presence, those hazel eyes opened. "You're back," she said around a sleepy yawn.

"I just got back." He held up the paper bag. "And I've got us a pregnancy test."

Still looking groggy, she sat up, took the bag from him, then peeked inside. "Austin, there are three tests in here."

"Never hurts to be sure, Dinah."

She pulled out one of the boxes. "I guess it doesn't, even though it says here that each test is ninety-nine-percent accurate."

"Mistakes happen."

"I suppose they do," she said softly.

"Let's go do this." He led the way to the bathroom. The moment she walked in, he started opening one of the boxes.

She snatched it right back. "Hold up, cowboy. We are definitely not taking this little test together. I'll be peeing on this stick in privacy."

He supposed she had a point. "Fine, but come right out. We'll do the waiting together."

Her expression looked pensive as she nodded. Then closed the door firmly on him.

Not wanting to wait on the other side of the door—that was creepy—Austin crossed the small space to the kitchenette. Standing among the polished white cabinets and counters, eyeing the dish towels with pink flowers printed on the edges, he realized he didn't mind being in the middle of all this femininity at all.

If they had a baby girl, being around all kinds of things that were pink and pretty could be his future. Funny, he kept expecting to feel the hard knot of panic in his insides. But all he felt was anticipation.

Which of course made him realize that Dinah expecting his baby wouldn't signal the end of the road for him. Instead, it felt as if her pregnancy would give him a whole new fresh start. No longer would he feel as if his future was covered with roadblocks because of who he was or what he'd done.

A child of his own meant a whole wealth of opportunities were in his future. Love and tears and laughter. Happiness.

But would Dinah even feel the same way? She might sleep with him, but that was a long way from wanting to carry his baby…and wanting him in her life. And what about her feelings? He knew she was important to him. He cared about Dinah, and he wanted her to be in his life whether or not she carried his baby.

But Dinah had never hinted that she felt that way about him. Now plagued by doubts, he felt green to the gills as the bathroom door opened.

She was holding the plastic stick as if it was about to explode in her hands.

He pointed to the counter. "Set it down, honey. We'll wait together."

Without a bit of argument, she did as he asked before moving to his side. "What are we going to do if I am pregnant?"

Every week in church, he'd prayed for strength. Prayed to be a better person. Prayed to be the man that he'd used to dream about becoming.

Now here he was being given the opportunity to be that man and so much more. If he didn't mess it up. "Well, I know what I'd like to do," he said.

"What's that?"

Dinah looked so worried. And so wary of that stick, he couldn't help but reach for her and pull her close. In one smooth move, he turned them both so their backs were facing the counter.

"Austin? What do you want to do?"

He swallowed hard. "How long does the box say we wait?"

"Three minutes."

"Okay." Looking into her eyes, seeing the doubt there, mixed with hope, he knew it was time to be completely honest. "Dinah, what I would like to do is marry you."

A whole wealth of emotions crossed her face. "If I'm pregnant."

He knew he wasn't going to get away without saying everything that was in his heart. He prayed that the road ahead of them really was filled with light and open doors. "I want to marry you no matter what, Dinah."

"Austin?"

"See, it's like this, D. I love you."

Her lips parted, whether because she was so overcome by emotion or shock, he didn't know.

"Dinah, if you're not carrying my baby, we can wait until

you're comfortable with the idea. That is, if you one day want to marry me, too."

She opened her mouth, then shut it again just as quickly. As if she was worried about saying the right thing.

"Dinah, just say it," he urged. "There's nothing you could say that is going to frighten me off."

"Austin, did you just ask me to marry you? Did you just propose?"

Okay, maybe she *could* say something that would still surprise the heck out of him! "I did." He rubbed his neck. "I'll be honest, I always kind of thought I'd have a ring first and be down on one knee. But I'm asking."

She paled. "I think I need a Snickers bar. You didn't happen to pick up any of those, did you?"

There again was that vulnerability that drew him to her like a bee to honey. "I'm sorry, I didn't. But if I would've known you wanted one, I would have bought you a slew of them." And, he mentally added, some decent food.

"Three pregnancy tests…a slew of Snickers bars." Her lips curved. "You don't do anything halfway, do you?"

"Never have."

And that was the truth, wasn't it? Never had he only messed up a little. He'd messed up so many things with his drinking. And his efforts to guard his heart had almost messed up his relationship with Cheyenne and her girls.

And with Dinah.

After they'd stood in silence for thirty seconds, old doubts surfaced again.

Had he made her uncomfortable? Had he inadvertently messed everything up, all over again? Worried, he cast an anxious glance her way. "Dinah? You think we can turn around now and look at that little stick?" He was about to go crazy from not knowing.

She bit her lip. "I'm not sure if I'm ready. Everything you said was so wonderful. What if I'm not?"

Not giving either of them another two seconds to think, he reached for her chin, turned her to face him and kissed her breathless. In his arms, Dinah didn't even hesitate. She melded her body to his, curving her arms around his neck. Feeling so sweet. So perfect.

When he lifted his head to draw a breath, she tried to argue. So he did the only thing he could. He kissed her again. And yet again, she followed his lead.

He couldn't resist the pull of satisfaction he felt. Dinah Hart didn't bend her will to anyone—except him, it seemed. Just like he wanted to bend for her. Gently rubbing his thumb along the fine lines of her cheekbones, he gazed into her lovely hazel eyes. "Better?"

"Um…no."

"No?"

"Austin, you didn't answer my question."

"I thought I did. If you're pregnant, I'm going to kiss you senseless. And if you're not, I'm going to kiss you senseless, too." He waggled his brows. "But then I might pull you to my bed and make everything last a little longer."

"But what about marriage?"

She looked so miserable, so torn, he almost laughed. "Dinah Hart, I love you. I want you to be happy. We'll figure it out."

"You think it's that easy?"

"I do," he said, figuring that he'd just learned something pretty important. If Dinah was tongue-tied or unsure? Take charge and kiss her. He leaned in, bussed her cheek, then curved his palms around her shoulders. "Now, here we go. One, two, three. Turn."

Obediently, she turned. Then she gasped.

And he made good on his promise and kissed her until they could hardly breathe.

Chapter Twenty-Five

Dinah stared at the test wand and swallowed hard. "Think we should do another test, just to be sure? I mean, we have three."

"I think we should do whatever you want." Austin looked a little pale.

"Are you upset?"

"Not at all." Wrapping his arms around her, he held her close. "I'm happy, Dinah. I couldn't be happier."

She looked at the plus sign on the pink plastic wand and felt tears start to well in her eyes. "Years ago, thinking about being pregnant sounded like the worst thing in the world to imagine. I was afraid to disappoint everyone. And afraid to disappoint myself."

"But now?"

"But now...I can't help but feel excited. Hopeful." Wary, she glanced his way.

"I feel exactly the same way," he said, dispelling all her worries. "I love you, Dinah. I love you and I want this baby with you."

That was Austin. Simple words, direct to her heart. Which made it all the easier to speak from her heart, as well. "I love you, too."

He closed his eyes. "You've made me so very happy."

"Really?" She still couldn't get over the fact that this was happening.

"Dinah, I couldn't be happier." Reaching out, he linked his fingers through hers. "Now, what would you like to do?"

"Can we go to the ranch and tell my mom?"

"Together?"

She nodded. "I'm excited, Austin."

"Then that's what we'll do. As soon as you eat something."

"I'm okay—"

"You're going to have to get used to this, D. I'm going look after you, and I intend to do a good job of it."

Looking into his blue eyes, she saw resolve and trust, and love. Those three things were so good, there was no way she was going to even think about fighting him. "All right, Austin."

A slow smile lit his face. "I knew I was going to like taking care of you. Now, you go get cleaned up and I'm going to make you something to eat."

Dinah did exactly as he suggested. She was beginning to discover that sometimes a person won by letting the other person get his way.

ALL THAT RESOLVE STARTED to melt away when they arrived at the ranch, however. Suddenly, she was seventeen all over again and desperate for her mother's approval.

"Things seem pretty quiet around here," she murmured when they got out of his truck. "I wonder where everyone is."

Austin looked around, then pointed to the barn. "Let's head over there. I think I hear voices."

"I bet everybody's checking out Midnight."

Sure enough, after walking through the main door, they passed the tack and feed rooms to the left, and her mother's office on the right. Standing inside the room was Colt's wife. "Hey, Leah."

She put down the paper she was scanning and grinned. "Hi, you two. Did you come to see Midnight?"

"We came to see everyone. But I'd love to see Midnight, too."

"How's he doing?" Austin asked as they continued walking toward the line of stalls...and the group of people crowded around one of the small corals just outside the back of the barn.

"He's amazing."

That was high praise, coming from Leah. "Amazing?" Dinah murmured.

Leah grinned. "You should see him! Everyone's watching him practically prance around the corral. Though Fancy Gal in the next corral is giving him something of a cold shoulder."

Austin chuckled. Wrapping an arm around her shoulders, he pressed his lips to Dinah's temple. "Now, isn't that just like a woman?"

Leah grinned. "If my guy had taken off for parts unknown without so much as a phone call, why, I'd be acting like Fancy Gal, too, if you want to know the truth. That horse has sure given us a heck of a lot of worry."

"He's definitely a horse with a mind of his own," Dinah said. Looking at Fancy, she said, "How's she doing, by the way?"

"She's doing well, carrying Midnight's young." Leah smiled. "I think she's a very happy momma."

"Is that right?" Austin murmured, pressing yet another kiss to Dinah's temple.

Leah looked at the two of them with narrowed eyes. For the first time, she seemed to notice the way Austin was holding Dinah. And the way she was enjoying being held.

"Wait a minute," she said slowly. "Y'all didn't come to visit Midnight, did you?"

"Not exactly. I came to visit with my mom." Dinah bit her lip and looked cautiously at Austin. "I hadn't thought about everyone being here, too. Maybe now's not the best time?"

Slipping his arm from her shoulders, he traipsed his fingers along her arm, coming to a stop when he curved his hand around her own. "I think it's the perfect time."

Leah raised her brows. "I was going to go back inside and work on payroll, but on second thought? I think I'll join you."

As they walked out to the coral, Dinah tried to quell her nerves. *What's done is done,* she told herself. *Even if your family isn't happy, it doesn't mean they are right.*

Her mother noticed her approach and gave them a little wave. "Dinah, Austin, just look at our guy. He's acting like he owns the place."

Dinah stared at Midnight and couldn't help but agree. The beautiful stallion raised his head, whinnied a bit, then trotted about with tons of self-confidence, each hoof practically stomping the ground. He knew he was the center of everyone's attention, and he seemed perfectly content to let them all admire him.

As Midnight continued to prance and pose, Colt whistled low. "That horse is practically begging to perform in the next rodeo."

"Maybe," Ace murmured. "He's definitely acting full of himself." Looking at Austin, Ace turned more serious. "Your father has a real way with Midnight."

"I do believe he enjoyed being with the horse," Austin said soberly. "I think the two of them have had their share of hardships."

After looking at their mom, Ace cleared his throat. "If, say, Buddy ever wanted to come out here and help with Midnight, we'd obliged."

Austin stilled. "Truly?"

"Heck, yeah. There's something about your dad that calms this guy. They've formed a bond that I don't want to breach. Midnight's had enough of those in his life, I think."

"I'll ask my dad, but I do believe he feels the same way

about Midnight as the horse feels about him. For some reason, they're a good pair."

Her brother grinned, then turned back to the horse. Austin turned to watch Midnight, too.

Though her stomach was sore from being sick all morning, Dinah was able to forget about her nerves for a few minutes as she squeezed into the spot along the fence that the family had made for her. "He really is beautiful," she said.

"The best," Ace agreed.

A few minutes later, Midnight gave a snort, then wandered toward the back of the coral. Now that his show was over, he seemed content to graze.

One by one, everyone moved from the fence.

Her mother stepped closer and looked her up and down. "Dinah, are you okay? You seem a little different."

On the other side of her mom, Colt inhaled sharply, but a dark look from Austin seemed to quell whatever he'd been ready to say.

"I'm fine," Dinah said. "But I have something I need to talk to you about."

"Dinah?" Now she'd gotten Ace's attention, too. "What's going on? Are you still worried about your case?"

"No…" Dinah looked from Austin to Colt to Ace to her mom. Just a few steps away, Flynn and Leah were listening. Waiting. Perhaps there was no time like the present to make things right. To make things better for her future and to finally make peace with the past.

Austin leaned close, wrapping his hands around her waist. "We don't have to do this now," he murmured into her ear. "There's no hurry."

"Wait a minute," Ace said. "No hurry about what?"

"You always did have good hearing, Ace," Dinah chided. "Too good."

"I needed them with you. When you were little, you'd try to get away with murder."

"Hey!"

Colt folded his arms over his chest. "A china teapot bring back any memories, little sister?"

She could feel her face flushing. "You knew?"

"Dinah, I think it would be best if we got everything out in the open," her mother said.

"All right. Austin and I are getting married."

After that bombshell, everyone looked a little stunned. Well, except for Colt. He looked pleased.

"Come on, Dinah. Say the rest. Y'all are getting married because…" Colt nudged. Completely ignoring Austin's dark scowl.

"Because we're in love. And because I'm pregnant," she said. In the next breath, she shook a finger at her big brother. Just as if she was five years old all over again. "And don't you say a word about this, Ace. You're not perfect, either."

He held up his hands as Flynn walked to stand next to him. "I wasn't about to."

As her mother seemed to do her best to get over her shock, Dinah gripped Austin's hands, still firmly around her waist.

"Mom, are you okay?"

"I've long stopped trying to run your lives. I can only hope that you're happy. Are you happy?"

"We are," she said, realizing that she was completely right. She was very happy right now.

"Then I'm happy, too."

"When's the wedding, Wright?" Colt asked.

"Just as soon as Dinah here gives me half a chance to do things right," Austin said.

Dinah cocked her head to one side. "Right?"

"You deserve this, D. I'm going to give you the ring and

the wedding you've always wanted. I'm going to give you the life you've always wanted."

As she thought about the things she used to want, and the things she used to think she needed in order to finally be happy, Dinah smiled.

"I already have it," she said. Feeling completely at peace for the first time in a long while. "Right now, I have everything I need. I have almost all of my family here, I have a life I love, and I have a man I love, a man who I've loved for practically forever. That's the way it's meant to be. I couldn't be happier."

And that was surely the truth.

* * * * *

The HARTS OF THE RODEO *miniseries
continues next month with Marin Thomas's book
BEAU: COWBOY PROTECTOR!*

When Forever, Texas's newest deputy, Gabe Rodriguez, rescues a woman from the scene of an accident, he encounters a mystery, as well.

Here's a sneak peek at A FOREVER CHRISTMAS by USA TODAY bestselling author Marie Ferrarella, available November 2012 from Harlequin® American Romance®.

It was still raining. Not nearly as bad as it had been earlier, but enough to put out what there still was of the fire. Mick was busy hooking up his tow truck to what was left of the woman's charred sedan and Alma was getting back into her Jeep. Neither one of them saw the woman in Gabe's truck suddenly sit up as he started the vehicle.

"No!"

The single word tore from her lips. There was terror in her eyes, and she gave every indication that she was going to jump out of the truck's cab—or at least try to. Surprised, Gabe quickly grabbed her by the arm with his free hand.

"I wouldn't recommend that," he told her.

The fear in her eyes remained. If anything, it grew even greater.

"Who are you?" the blonde cried breathlessly. She appeared completely disoriented.

"Gabriel Rodriguez. I'm the guy who pulled you out of your car and kept you from becoming a piece of charcoal."

Her expression didn't change. It was as if his words weren't even registering. Nonetheless, Gabe paused, giving her a minute as he waited for her response.

But the woman said nothing.

"Okay," he coaxed as he drove toward the town of Forever, "your turn."

The world, both inside the moving vehicle and outside of it, was spinning faster and faster, making it impossible for her to focus on anything. Moreover, she couldn't seem to pull her thoughts together. Couldn't get past the heavy hand of fear that was all but smothering her.

"My turn?" she echoed. What did that mean, her turn? Her turn to do what?

"Yes, your turn," he repeated. "I told you my name. Now you tell me yours."

Her name.

The two words echoed in her brain, encountering only emptiness. Suddenly very weary, she strained hard, searching, waiting for something to come to her.

But nothing did.

The silence stretched out. Finally, just before he repeated his question again, she said in a small voice, hardly above a whisper, "I can't."

Who is this mystery woman?
Find out in A FOREVER CHRISTMAS
by Marie Ferrarella, coming November 2012
from Harlequin® American Romance®.